"Her Christmas Snowman"
The Gingerbread Lane #1
By Laura Ann

HER CHRISTMAS HANDYMAN

First edition. November 23, 2020.

Written by Laura Ann.

DEDICATION

Every first book is dedicated to my husband.
Without your support, I never would have dared to dream.

ACKNOWLEDGEMENTS

No author works alone. Thank you, Brenda.
You make it Christmas every time
I get a new cover. And thank you to my Beta Team.
Truly, your help with my stories is immeasurable.

CHAPTER 1

Hope blew out a long breath, using her air to push her bangs out of her face as she trudged up the last few steps of her grandmother's mansion. A cold breeze swirled through the night, making her nose drip and sending a shiver down her spine. If it wasn't for the warm, welcoming lights coming from inside the Cliffside Bed and Breakfast, lovingly known as the Gingerbread Inn to the town's inhabitants, then Hope would be hightailing it back into town and finding a warm corner to read a book in.

After graduating from college with a masters in English last spring, Hope never expected to still be jobless, nor did she expect her Grandma Claire to have an accident that required hip surgery. During her recovery, Grandma Claire had to shut down her family legacy, the bed and breakfast that she ran on the coast in Oregon. Now that Grandma was home, she wanted to open again for Christmas, but needed help.

With the rest of the family busy in their individual lives, help had arrived by way of Hope and two of her cousins, who were hopefully already inside. Shivering in her new winter boots, Hope prayed that her cousin Emory would have some hot chocolate waiting for her.

"HOPE!" Isabella, or Bella, cried out, throwing open the front door and embracing her cousin. "I'm so glad you're here," Bella whispered as she continued to hug Hope tightly. Bella stepped back, a wide smile on her round face. "It's going to be just like old times!" she squealed, doing a little bounce on her toes.

Hope laughed lightly and wiped her feet on the rug. "One big slumber party, huh? Is that the plan?"

Bella laughed. "If we can convince Emory that she doesn't have to get up at four thirty in the morning to bake, then we might be able to pull it off."

Hope shivered again. "Geez. I'm glad I'm not a baker," she mumbled.

"Here. Let me take that." Bella grabbed Hope's suitcase. "Is this all you brought?" Bella asked incredulously. "You do realize we're going to be here for, like, a whole month at least?"

Hope frowned. "Uh...yeah. Why would I need more?"

Bella blew a raspberry through her lips. "I have three times as many suitcases and Emory brought two with kitchen supplies alone." She grinned. "Don't worry. We'll make a fashionista out of you yet."

Hope resisted the urge to roll her eyes. She had no desire to be a fashionista. Her jeans, blouses and cardigans were comfortable and practical. She planned to be a teacher or a librarian. Why in the world did she need to carry enough clothes with her to fill a warehouse? Hope shook her head. *Bella can be the fashionable one. I'll stick with my favorite accessories...books.*

"Hope? Is that you, dear?"

Hope smiled, left her luggage at the door and hurried through the foyer and into the large sitting room of the mansion. "Grandma!"

"There you are!" Grandma Claire held out her arms with a wide smile, waiting for Hope to come to her.

The fact that she stayed sitting down only reminded Hope of her grandmother's surgery. She looked the older woman over, noting the slightly pale skin and the lack of Grandma Claire's signature bun. Grandma Claire's white hair was braided to the side of her head, a hairdo that was probably far easier to create, but took away the 'Mrs. Santa Claus' look she had worn for as long as Hope could remember.

"How are you?" Hope asked softly as she gently hugged her grandmother.

"Just dandy," Grandma Claire responded. She leaned back to look Hope in the face. "At least I will be when my ridiculous doctor lets me do more."

Hope grinned and shook her head. *Leave it to Grandma to want to be on the move.* "You're doctor isn't ridiculous," she said. "He wants you to heal, and so do we. That's why we're here."

Grandma Claire patted Hope's cheek. "And that's the best thing to come out of this injury."

Hope straightened and looked to Bella. "Where's Emory?"

Bella opened her mouth, but another voice beat her in answering.

"I'm here," Emory said, walking into the room with a tray in her arms. She smiled warmly at Hope. "I figured you'd be hungry when you arrived."

"You're an angel," Hope breathed, walking over to her other cousin. The three girls had all grown up together and were often called 'the triplets' by family members, though they looked very little alike.

Hope had blond hair, while Emory was a true brunette. Bella's strawberry blonde came in somewhere in the middle. Their builds were just as different. While Hope and Emory were of similar heights, Hope's curves showed that she didn't have a relationship with exercise, while Emory's willowy figure showed off all the time spent doing yoga. Bella had the biggest personality, but was several inches shorter than the other women, coming in at a grand five-foot-two.

The only attribute the girls had in common were the blue Simmons eyes. The cornflower blue color was distinctive and a strong enough trait that most of the family had it, including Grandma Claire.

"Mmm..." Hope hummed as she chewed the warm chocolate biscotti that Emory had on the tray. "This is amazing." She paused. "I already gained ten pounds during the last semester of my degree." She playfully glared at her cousin. "I was hoping to fit back into my pants while I was here."

Emory smirked. "It's Christmas. I make no promises not to use heavy cream and butter in abundance."

"That's what I'm afraid of," Hope moaned. Laughing together, the cousins embraced. "Good to see you," Hope said.

"You too," Emory replied. "This month will be fun."

Hope stepped back. "I hope so." She smiled at her grandmother and Bella, who was sitting next to the older woman. "Being here is definitely better than spending the holidays alone in my tiny apartment."

Bella snorted. "You need to get out more. Your book boyfriends are good in theory, but they can't kiss you under the mistletoe."

Hope felt her cheeks heat up. She wasn't as people-oriented as Bella was, which was easy to see in the fact that Bella wanted to be a journalist. She always wanted to be on the front lines and had no fear of strangers.

"Don't start," Emory sighed, grabbing a mug and walking it over to Grandma Claire. "We're here to help Grandma, not to bicker about our love lives."

"What love lives?" Bella pouted, folding her arms over her chest.

"The one that would get in the way of me opening my bakery," Emory shot back.

Hope grinned. It was nice to know that Emory was on her side. A boyfriend sounded nice, but Hope had no idea where she would meet someone. She spent her time subbing in multiple schools, only being around for a few days before she was reassigned. That made meeting someone at work near impossible. And since she didn't go anywhere else, her options were limited to say the least.

"Never give up hope, my dears," Grandma Claire said with a soft smile as she accepted the mug of cocoa. "The Gingerbread Inn has magic of its own." She pumped her eyebrows up and down. "And it's Christmas. You never know what will happen."

"Claire?"

All four heads swiveled toward the deep, smooth tone.

Hope felt her jaw fall slack as a handsome, dark-haired man stepped into the room. A tool belt sat low on his hips and a tight T-shirt stretched across his chest. He oozed masculinity, and it struck Hope right in the gut.

"ENOCH?" BELLA ASKED uncertainly. "Enoch Dunlap?"

Enoch tilted his head and grinned. "Guilty as charged." He studied the pretty redhead in front of him before inspiration dawned. "Oh, right!" He snapped his fingers. "Claire told me her granddaughters were coming." He smiled easily and looked around at all the women. His gaze stuttered and got caught for a second on a beautiful blonde across the room. She looked slightly shell-shocked, but her wide blue eyes and curvy figure were enough to catch any man's attention.

He forced himself to go back to the woman who had spoken to him. "Isabella, right?"

She stood and smiled. "Just Bella, but wow. Good memory." Bellla stepped forward to shake his hand. "Good to see you again. What's it been, like ten years?"

He rubbed the back of his neck uncomfortably as it grew hot. "Something like that. About the time I graduated high school and left town." He couldn't seem to help but glance at the blonde again. Her name was eluding him and it was frustrating.

"Obviously you came back," Bella said, putting her hands on her hips and drawing the conversation back her way.

She's not gonna let me off easy, is she? he thought. He wanted to talk to the other woman, but Bella seemed intent on conversation. Enoch turned to Bella with wide eyes and nodded again. "Uh, yeah. Been back a couple of years."

"He works full-time for the inn," Grandma Claire interjected. "He's the resident handyman."

"I thought you had to let everyone go when you closed the inn while you recovered?" another of the granddaughters asked with a frown.

Grandma nodded. "I did. All except Enoch." She smiled lovingly at him. "He's like a member of the family and without his amazing touch, this old house would be in ruins by now."

Heat flushed up Enoch's cheeks, but he smiled back at the woman who was like a mother to him. Then turning to the one who had spoken, he wracked his brain for her name. He remembered it was something unusual. "Emory, right?" Enoch asked, stepping forward to shake her hand as well.

"Yep. Good job," Emory said. She glanced at the tray and back. "Want a hot chocolate? We were all enjoying a little treat."

"If that's the wonderful smell that's been tempting me for the last half-hour, then definitely," he joked, smelling the air for effect.

"Oh, that's the biscotti," Emory corrected as she hurried out of the room. "Just let me grab another plate."

"Don't go to any...trouble," he trailed off as Emory disappeared. He turned and smiled sheepishly at the blonde. "I didn't mean to put her out."

"Oh, you're not," Bella piped up from where she'd sat back down. She waved a hand in the air. "Emory lives for this kind of thing."

Enoch nodded but his eyes stayed on quiet one. "I don't quite remember your name, but I think it was some kind of virtue."

The woman's smile fell and Enoch held back a wince. *Way to go, buddy. Nothing says 'I want to get to know you more' like 'I can't remember your name'.*

She cleared her throat. "Hope."

Enoch nodded vigorously, feeling awkward. "That's right. I knew I should have remembered it." He offered his hand, which she took reluctantly. Her small fingers felt soft and just the right size.

She went to pull away, but Enoch couldn't quite bring himself to just let go. Holding his grip slightly longer than was polite, he let his fingers slide along her warm palm. "It's good to see you again, Hope," he said softly, his voice having gone slightly husky. "What have you been up to these past years?"

Hope blinked rapidly, not answering him right away, and Enoch began to think he'd insulted her worse than he'd thought.

"She's an English teacher," Bella said, her voice distracted.

He looked over his shoulder and saw that Bella was scrolling on her phone. "That totally makes sense," Enoch said easily. He turned back to Hope. "You always did have your head in a book, if I recall correctly."

Enoch ignored Bella's snort and saw a smile grace Hope's soft pink lips. "That's right."

Enoch made a point of looking around, then leaned conspiratorially. "Don't tell anyone, cause you know, it might ruin my reputation, but I've been known to devour a good book now and again myself."

Hope's smile grew. "You like to read?"

"Shhh!" he teased, patting the air with his hand.

Hope laughed and Enoch was entranced by the sound. *So the bookworm grew up. Who'd have thought?*

"I won't tell anyone," she said, zipping her lips with her fingers.

"Good. It can be our secret," Enoch said with a wink.

"One hot chocolate and two slices of biscotti," Emory said as she reentered the room, completely oblivious to the flirting going on.

Enoch walked over and picked up the plate with a biscuity-looking thing on it. He eyed it warily, but the smells coming from it were completely tantalizing, so he risked a bite. Sweet, warm chocolate and crisp cookie met his taste buds and they began to rejoice. "This is amazing," Enoch said, swallowing a mouthful. "Thank you."

Emory nodded. "You're welcome." With a polite smile, Emory disappeared again.

"Did I say something wrong?" Enoch asked, turning to look at Hope.

She pinched her lips between her teeth, as if to keep from laughing, then shook her head. "Nope. Nothing."

Enoch frowned. "What's so funny?"

"You've uh, got a..." Hope motioned across her lip and Enoch mimicked her actions, then groaned when he figured it out.

"Well, that's a great first impression," he grumbled, completely mortified.

"Here, hon," Grandma Claire said, reaching out with a napkin. "And don't worry," she whispered loudly. "I think you did just fine."

CHAPTER 2

S till slightly amused, Hope walked to the chair opposite her grandmother and sat down.

"Well..." Enoch put his hands on his hips. "That stair rail is done and the leak is gone in the powder room."

"Wonderful," Grandma Claire said. "I couldn't do this without you."

Enoch grinned. "Let's not get too gushy, shall we? Your granddaughters might get jealous."

Hope laughed, along with Grandma and Bella.

"So what brought you back to Seagull Cove?" Bella asked, crossing one leg over the other. "How long have you worked for Grandma? Do you have a family?"

Enoch put his hands up. "Better slow down or I won't be able to answer everything."

"He doesn't need to tell us his life story," Hope scolded her cousin, feeling completely foolish that she hadn't thought about the fact that Enoch might be taken. Here she was, ogling him like a young teenage girl, and he might have a wife and child at home. Though, the way he caressed her hand made her think otherwise.

"It's all right," Enoch said. He walked over to the couch and settled in. "But fair's fair. If I answer the questions, you have to do the same."

"Deal," Bella immediately said and shot a triumphant look at Hope.

Hope sighed but nodded.

"Okay, let me see if I remember everything you asked," he said thoughtfully. "When life in the big city ended up killing my creative spirit, I packed up my few possessions and came back with my tail between my legs," Enoch said with a self-deprecating laugh. "I've been working for Claire for about...what?" he directed at her. "Two years?"

"Sounds about right," Grandma Claire nodded.

Hope found herself frowning. *Why was he coming back with his tail between his legs? Was there a problem at home? What was he doing that required creativity?*

Enoch nodded in return. "And no, I don't have a family, other than Clair here." His eyes went to Hope. "Your turn."

Hope felt her eyes go wide. "Mine?" she squeaked.

Enoch laughed. "Yeah. Yours. Where have you been teaching?" he asked. "And how did you manage to get off long enough to come help around here?"

Hope swallowed hard. "Uh...I'm not really teaching. I just finished my masters this last summer and haven't, uh..." Shame burned through her at her next admission. "I haven't been able to find a job yet, so I'm just subbing wherever I can."

Enoch nodded. "Good for you. What grade do you want to teach?"

"High school," she responded.

"She also writes," Bella piped up.

Enoch's eyebrows shot up. "Yeah? You have anything published?"

Hope shrugged her shoulders. "Not yet. I haven't finished anything to send in, but I'm thinking about it."

"It sounds perfect for you," Enoch said. "At least from what I can remember of you." He smiled. "And what about your family?"

"My...what?"

"Do you have a husband? Boyfriend? Significant other?" Enoch teased.

Hope quickly shook her head. "Uh...nope. Just me."

Enoch relaxed back in his seat with a smile.

Hope could have sworn she heard him mutter something like 'perfect', but she wasn't sure, and she didn't dare hope. *I'm only here for a month. What can happen in that amount of time?*

"How about you, Bella? Have an interesting story to tell?" Enoch asked, reminding Hope that she wasn't the only female in the room.

"I always have a story to tell," Bella quipped. "I have a degree in journalism and one day you'll see my face plastered on a billboard on the highway with a Pulitzer Prize next to my head."

Enoch burst out laughing and Hope swooned just a little. She needed a recording of the sound so she could listen to it when she was sitting in her apartment all by herself. It was absolutely swoon-worthy and would help take her mind off her bills.

"I look forward to saying I knew you when," Enoch answered. "Where are you working?"

Bella scrunched up her nose. "I'm independent. I've sent in articles to places but haven't been picked up as a regular yet." She grinned. "I'm interested in crime reporting, so it's a smaller niche."

"Wow," Enoch responded. "No queasy stomach for you, huh?"

"Absolutely not," Bella said firmly. "I find it all fascinating."

Hope shook her head. "You can keep it," she stated. "I'll stick to the books."

"One day I'll tell you the real stories, and you and I can write a thriller together," Bella said with a grin. "I'll even let you add in some romance if you ask nicely."

"Romance?" Enoch asked, his right eyebrow slowly rising. "That's what you like to write about?"

Hope ducked her chin a little. Could she help it if romance novels were her weakness? Who would turn down those hunky men who always knew exactly what to say?

Grandma reached over to pat her hand. "Wars have been fought over love, sweetie. It makes everything better." She winked. "You get that enjoyment from me."

Hope smiled gratefully at her grandmother. She would never complain about having something in common with her. Grandma Claire was the type of woman everyone should aspire to be.

"Amen to that," Enoch inserted. "My mother went through those things like candy."

Hope smiled at him. "Thanks," she said softly.

He smiled back. "Let me know when your book is out. If I'm going to have a bunch of famous friends, I'm going to take shameless advantage."

They all laughed just as Emory came back into the sitting room. "What's so funny?" she asked, shuffling the empty dishes on the tray.

"We're telling life stories," Enoch replied. "What about you?"

"What about me?"

"Where are you working? Do you have a family? What are your life plans?"

Emory frowned. "Wow. You guys got totally deep in the few minutes I was gone."

Hope smiled. Emory was a down-to-earth workaholic and it showed in her conversations. She found her eyes drifting to Enoch. *What exactly is he? He's been charming and sweet tonight, but is that just because we're new? Will he be attracted to one of my cousins? Flirtatious Bella, or hard-working Emory? Can he tell I'm drooling over here as I watch him?* She sighed quietly. *This is why I stay away from dating. It's way too hard to figure out what people are thinking.*

ENOCH WAS COMPLETELY relaxed on the couch as he listened to the women chatter and laugh, but even so, he found that every part of him was ardently in tune with Hope. When she smiled, he smiled. When she laughed, he heard it. He found himself waiting for her voice in the conversation, though she appeared to be the quietest of all the cousins.

It meant that trying to get to know her was going to be a little more difficult. *I bet that if I got her alone, she'd open up. She doesn't appear shy...just quiet.*

"Any idea where you want the storefront to be?" Enoch threw out, hoping he wasn't too out of the conversation.

Emory pursed her lips. "I don't know. I mean, I'm in Seattle right now, but I'm open to somewhere else. There's already an overabundance of specialty bakeries in the King County area." She shrugged. "When I have the money to get going, I'll look into it more. Right now I'm in save mode, so it doesn't matter."

Enoch nodded. "Sounds like you ladies have it all figured out."

Grandma Claire smiled. "These three were always bright go-getters." Her eyes misted slightly. "Just like their mothers."

Hope reached over and grabbed her grandma's hand. "Who were just like *their* mother."

"Oh," Grandma Claire scolded playfully, wiping at the corner of her eye. "Look at me. Old age seems to make me weepy." She laughed. "And I don't like it."

"My grandma used to say it was because you had so many more emotions stored up by the time you got to that age," Enoch offered. He smiled warmly. He couldn't imagine what his life would be like without Claire. He'd left Seagull Cove in a huff, an eighteen-year-old who knew everything. But when his plans had died, he'd come home to nothing.

His dad had refused to acknowledge him since graduation and even though Enoch had tried to reopen their communication, nothing had come from it. *It's amazing how well a drunk man can hold a grudge when half the time he can't remember what day it is,* Enoch mused, his thoughts taking a dark turn.

"Enoch, dear, are you feeling like everything is in place for tomorrow?" Claire asked, her question bringing him out of the past.

He nodded, grateful for her interruption. "Yep. As far as I can tell, nothing is broken...at the moment."

Hope frowned. "Do things break that often around here?" She looked slightly worried, her eyes darting between Claire and himself.

Enoch smiled and shook his head. "The house is over a hundred years old. Things break down all the time, but don't worry," he hurried to add, "it's mostly little things like leaks, dents...stuck window frames. Big stuff doesn't come up very often."

She nodded, looking relieved.

"Although, there have been more breakdowns than normal," Enoch mused, rubbing his stubbly chin. *Note to self, better shave now that the women are here.*

Bella tilted her head, curiosity lighting her gaze. "Really? What do you think is going on? Is the weather worse than normal?"

"Poppycock," Claire interrupted, waving a hand in the air. "The older the house gets, the more we're going to find problems." She pointed a finger at Enoch. "Don't go filling my girls' heads with ghost stories, mister. I hired you for your handyman skills, not to scare everybody."

Enoch chuckled and nodded. "Anything you say, Claire."

Bella pouted. "But I want to hear!"

Emory rolled her eyes and walked back out, carrying the tray. "Try not to break any headlines while we're here, huh, Bella? Our goal is to get the inn back on its feet and help Grandma heal. Not show up on the front page of the newspaper."

Bella scowled and folded her arms over her chest, but didn't speak any further.

Despite what Claire said, Enoch was worried about things, though he wouldn't press the matter. The fall Claire had taken a couple months ago should have never happened. She kept the house in shipshape order, though she only employed a few workers. It was her pride and joy, and the wet towel she'd stumbled on would have never been overlooked.

Either she's losing her memory or something funny is going. He hadn't told her that several of his tools had been moved as well. Showing up in places they never should have been. *Probably better to keep it to myself for now. I'll just take extra care to watch things.*

"Well..." Hope slapped her hands on her thighs. "I think maybe it's time to turn in for the night. I don't know about anything else, but I'm exhausted from the drive and could use a good night's sleep before everything begins tomorrow."

"That's a good plan," Claire agreed. She moved to stand up from her chair. Before Enoch could get over to assist her, Hope and Bella were at Claire's side.

Instead, he stood rocking back on his heels, wondering if he should interfere or not. He'd been helping Claire this whole time, but it was probably wise to let the women do it. Claire would prefer it.

"See you tomorrow," Enoch said as the women left the room with a wave. He let his eyes linger on Hope's figure as she walked beside Claire. She really was quite attractive, and her soft-spoken nature was enticing to him. He'd had enough conflict in his early years to last a lifetime and had worked hard to create a good, peaceful existence. The last thing he would ever want was to date a woman who was loud and boisterous.

Musing on the possibilities of getting Hope alone in order to learn more about her, he meandered to his apartment. The lights were off, which almost caused him to miss the shadow standing outside his doorway.

"Oh, hey, Trisha," he said as her face came into view. Her black hair made her blend into the shadows. Enoch stepped back a little, uncomfortable that she was so close. "What brings you here?" He'd known the woman since high school, and during the time that she'd been the housekeeper at the Gingerbread Inn, they'd spent a few lunch hours laughing and chatting together.

"Hey," she said with a wide smile. Her hands were stuffed in her jacket pockets and she shivered a little. "I had a little time on my hands this evening." She eyed his door. "I wondered if maybe you wanted to have a nightcap or something?"

Enoch shook his head. "You know I don't drink," he said softly, trying to let her down as nicely as possible. Though they'd worked together, Enoch had always worried that Trisha wanted more than he did, but she'd never pushed the issue and he'd never asked her out, so he'd assumed things were okay. Obviously that wasn't quite the case.

"I know." She shrugged, biting her lip. "But maybe you'd like some company?"

Enoch held back a sigh. "I don't think that's a good idea, Trisha. I appreciate your friendship, though." He lifted his eyebrows, desperate to change the subject. "How's the job hunting going? Anyone hiring?" Seagull Cove wasn't very large, so when Trisha lost her job during the inn closure, he worried she'd struggle to find a new one.

Her eyes were on her booted feet as she spoke. "Uh, I'm a clerk at the candy shop on First. It's only part-time right now, but they said it might be more when the busy season hits next summer."

"Wow, working in a candy store would be a dream come true," he encouraged with a chuckle. "Eating sweets all day long wouldn't be good for my figure though." He pinched his lips together, growing cold in the windy, wet weather. Enoch didn't dare open the door with her standing there, though. It would be too hard to keep her from coming in.

"You're welcome to come visit anytime," she offered hopefully.

"Yeah, I'll have to see what my schedule is like now that the inn is reopening," he said carefully.

She nodded and watched him from under her eyelashes. An awkward silence hung in the air before she smiled, though it was easy to tell it was forced. "Right. Well, I guess I'll head out, then. Have a good night."

"Night." Enoch watched her go, but didn't open his door until her taillights disappeared through the trees. Blowing out a long breath, he pushed a hand through his hair and walked inside, shaking for a moment as the heat massaged his skin. "Dodged a bullet there," he muttered to himself. "Hopefully that's the last of it."

CHAPTER 3

The next morning, Hope woke up and took a minute to adjust to her surroundings. The bed she was in was certainly not the same as her usual thin mattress and the air didn't nip at her nose because her tiny heater couldn't keep up.

Instead, she was toasty warm, lying on a cloud and surrounded by the scent of... She sniffed. *Is that cinnamon?* With a grin, she sat up. "Emory must have gotten up early," she murmured, daring to put her toe on the rug. When her foot didn't feel like it was going to get frostbite, Hope stood up and padded to the ensuite, where she took care of business.

Throwing her hair into a bun and pulling on a fluffy sweater, she worked her way downstairs and toward the kitchen. "Morning," she said as she entered, taking another long sniff of the delicious air.

"Good morning, sweetheart," Grandma Claire said from her seat at the table. "Did you sleep well?"

Hope kissed her grandmother's cheek. "Of course. You always did have the best beds here."

Grandma Claire chuckled. "That's what our guests say as well."

"Speaking of guests," Bella piped in as she entered the room. "Since today is the official reopening, do you already have any bookings?"

"Oh, goodness," Grandma Claire huffed. "I should have spoken to you girls about it already." She shook her head.

"Hey, it's no biggie, Grandma," Hope inserted. "We'll get everything taken care of."

"That's why we're here," Emory called out from her place at the stove.

"Why we're here is to eat those cinnamon rolls you have about to come out of the oven," Bella said, rubbing her hands together in gleeful anticipation.

"Only one," Emory retorted firmly. "I'm saving them for new arrivals."

"Where's the fun in that?" Bella whined.

While Grandma Claire chuckled, Hope sighed. *Why do all skinny people eat and never gain weight? All I have to do is look at a cinnamon roll and I put on five pounds.*

A pat to her hand brought Hope's attention back to her grandmother. "You're beautiful, dear," she whispered. "Don't let anyone tell you otherwise." She dropped her voice even more. "Besides, men like to have a little something to hold onto—"

"Oh my gosh, Grandma!" Hope gasped. She put a hand to her hot cheeks. "We are not having this conversation."

Grandma Claire shrugged nonchalantly. "Another day, then."

Or never, Hope thought. She shook her head.

"I mean it," Emory snapped.

Hope looked to see Bella teasing their cousin about the pastries. "Ladies..." Hope scolded. "Come on."

Bella grinned unrepentantly. "Can I help it if you bake such good stuff that I want some?"

"You *can* have some," Emory said with a sniff. "Just not all of them."

"With smells like that, stopping might be difficult." Enoch's deep voice broke through the feminine chatter, bringing the noise to a stop.

Hope froze in place. *What in the world is he doing here so early? Did I do my hair?* Slowly, in order not to bring attention to herself, she reached up and touched her top-not, then cringed at the feel of the messiness. *Oh my word. Why can't I just melt into the floor. I think that would be less painful than letting him see me like this.*

"Did I forget to tell you?" Grandma Claire whispered with a mischievous grin. "Enoch lives here. The apartment over the garage is his."

Hope squished her eyes shut and held in her groan.

"Are we going to get to see your handsome face every morning?" Bella chirped from her place next to Emory. "Can't say that I'd be opposed to that."

Hope started to glare at Bella, but stopped at the last minute when she realized Enoch was looking right at her. "Good morning," she whispered.

His smile was inviting, and suddenly Hope felt like that puddle she'd asked for might not be so far away. "Good morning. Sleep well?" His eyes drifted to her messy hair and his lips twitched, but the warmth in his eyes helped ease any sting of the teasing.

"A little too well," she quipped back, causing him to chuckle. Hope smiled at his reaction, enjoying the deep sound of his amusement.

"Your grandma does have a thing for good mattresses."

"Amen," Bella added.

"I'm not complaining," Emory threw over her shoulder, not looking away from her job of frosting the cinnamon rolls.

"But to answer your earlier question, I live here," Enoch said nonchalantly. He walked over to the table and sat across from Hope and Claire.

"Ooooh," Bella said, nodding her head slowly. "So this really is full-time."

Enoch nodded. "Yep."

"Wow, Hope," Bella said with a smirk. "Aren't we the lucky girls?"

Hope felt her cheeks flare again. *I guess my attraction hasn't gone unnoticed. Great. Bella will never let me live it down.*

"So what's on the agenda for today?" Enoch asked, grabbing an apple from the center of the table and taking a sharp bite.

"Hope, would you be a dear and grab the book from the front desk?" Grandma Claire asked.

"Of course." Hope darted out of the room, praying the blush on her cheeks would calm down before she got back. After arriving at the front desk, she looked around until she found the black binder her grandmother used to book reservations.

Tucking it under her arm, she took a deep breath, braced herself for more awkwardness, then headed back to the kitchen. "Here you go," Hope said with a forced smile. She handed Grandma Claire the book and sat down. "Mmm...thanks, Emory."

A plate with an oozing roll was at Hope's spot and Bella had joined them at the table. Emory was the only one not sitting. Instead, she flitted around the kitchen, muttering under her breath.

"Wonderful, thank you," Grandma Claire said with a smile. She took the binder and opened it, flipping to the right page. "We have three rooms booked starting today, and two more tomorrow. By the end of the week we're going to have all ten rooms full."

Hope whistled low. "Geez. Has the mansion been cleaned? Are we ready to go? What exactly do you want us to do?"

Enoch chuckled at her slew of questions. "Don't worry. Your grandma has things fairly well in hand." He winked. "Though I know she's grateful to have you all here."

Hope smiled and slunk into her seat a little, embarrassed at her outburst. "Sorry. I just want to make sure we're prepared."

"HE'S RIGHT," CLAIRE added. "I'm grateful you're here, but we should be able to move forward fairly easily. I paid a service to have the inn cleaned, so it should be ready to go, and Enoch, of course, keeps up with everything else." She smiled at him and he reciprocated. "I just need each of you to take on a job going forward," Claire finished.

"We already talked about that," Bella inserted, scraping her plate with her fork to get the last bit of icing. "I'm going to be doing the cleaning." She made a face. "Hope is going to run the front desk and Emory will run the kitchen." Bella rolled her eyes. "As if that was even a question."

Hope smiled understandingly. "I guess you could run the front desk, if you wanted," she said. "I don't mind doing the cleaning."

Bella pursed her lips. "I might take you up on that. Scrubbing toilets has never been my thing."

Enoch huffed quietly. He guessed that Bella just wanted to be in the middle of the action and the front desk would allow her to talk to more people.

"You're choice," Hope reiterated. "I can do whatever."

Bella shrugged. "Okay, I'll take it." She grinned. "That's where all the interesting things are found anyway."

Exactly what I thought. Enoch looked to Hope. *But having her do the housekeeping will actually give me a better chance at spending time with her, so I'm not going to complain.*

"That sounds just fine," Claire said, still looking through the book. "You'll probably be happier at the front desk anyway," she said, looking at Bella.

Bella grinned.

"Now that's something I haven't smelled in ages," came a masculine voice from the doorway.

"Good morning, Sheriff," Enoch said, leaning back in his seat. "Coming to test out the fresh-baked goods?" He peeked over to see Claire turning slightly red as she looked at the sheriff. Claire was a beautiful older woman, and had been widowed for ten years. For as long as he'd been working at the inn, Enoch had noticed a not-so-subtle attraction between the widowed sheriff and innkeeper. The two, however, had only ever flirted from afar, neither making a real move. It was equal parts frustrating and amusing to watch.

The sheriff took his cowboy hat off and nodded to each female in the room. "Claire," he said, his voice gruff. "Judging by the amount of summer skies looking at me, these must be your lovely granddaughters."

Claire's cheeks grew more red than before and Enoch saw the moment when Hope spotted the reaction. Her blue eyes shot to his and widened in surprise. Pinching her lips together, she purposefully shot her eyes to her grandmother, then the sheriff, and back to Enoch. Her question was clear.

Enoch gave her a subtle nod and Hope's jaw opened just slightly. He kept his chuckle quiet at her reaction.

"William," Claire said graciously, recovering her reaction to his arrival. "You are, indeed, correct. This is Hope Masterson. She's going to be my housekeeper for the next while. This is Isabella Wood, an aspiring journalist. She's going to run the front desk. And the delicious smells you're taking in, come from Emory's baking efforts. She'll be running the kitchen and chairing the gingerbread competition for Christmas."

Sheriff Davidson nodded again. "Ladies." He turned to Emory. "The Gingerbread Village is a big undertaking. You ready to take on the politics of that?"

Emory smirked. "I doubt it's worse than the competition at culinary school. That was pretty cutthroat."

Sheriff Davison smiled. "Well, Old Lady Pearson said she's back in it this year, so hold onto your garters and prepare for the worst. She's had it out for Ms. Claire, here, for ages."

Claire scowled while Enoch laughed. "That old biddy never could handle second place." She sniffed. "Can I help it if she can't see well enough to make lattice anymore?"

Bella snickered, but Hope frowned. "She can't be that bad," Hope said, glaring a little at her cousin's laughter.

"I hate to say it, but she is," Enoch added. "She's been second place for a long time and she's gotten more and more bitter about it each time. I wouldn't put anything past her at this point." He leaned forward. "She's the type of old lady who calls the police if you cut the corner on her grass."

Hope's frown deepened. "Really? I thought those kinds of people were only in books."

Enoch shook his head while the sheriff scoffed. "Nope. It's real. And she's right here in Seagull Cove."

Hope huffed. "Well then, I hope she stays in second place forever."

"Way to go, Hope!" Bella called out. "Stick it to the man...I mean, woman!"

Hope shook her head, but grinned. Her reaction only confirmed to Enoch even more that she was the type of person he wanted to get to know more. He'd known her when they were young, at least whenever the girls came to visit their grandmother. However, since he was a few years older, he'd graduated, moved away and hadn't seen them since. Knowing the bookworm she was as a young teenager didn't mean he knew anything about her as an adult, and it was beautiful, adult-Hope that he was the most eager to spend time with.

"Will you stay for breakfast, Sheriff?" Claire asked.

The sheriff shuffled his feet a little and clinched his hat. "I don't want to intrude."

"You're not intruding," Emory said decisively. She went back to the oven to dish up another cinnamon roll. "You were invited and I don't like my food to go bad." She walked over and set the plate on the table. "You might as well take advantage."

Enoch coughed and cleared his throat to hold back his laughter as the sheriff quickly took Emory up on her offer. It was clear that the granddaughters were intrigued by the sheriff and Claire's reaction to each other. It would be interesting to see if the women's presence helped push anything along in the slow-moving romance.

CHAPTER 4

"I need to go to the store to grab the candy for the gingerbread house," Emory stated as everyone finished their food.

"Ooh, that sounds fun," Bella said, jumping up from her seat. "I always love a good candy shop."

"You're running the front desk," Hope pointed out. She glanced at her watch. "And the phone lines open in fifteen minutes. You'll need to be available."

"Crud," Bella said, sinking back down. "Maybe I shouldn't have swapped you."

Hope opened her mouth to say she'd switch back, but Grandma spoke instead. "You'll do wonderful at it, dear," she said soothingly to Bella. "You have such fun speaking to people and the front desk is the best place to do that."

"Hope?" Emory asked, rapidly typing into her phone.

"Since Grandma said she already had the house cleaned, I suppose I don't have anything to do until tomorrow morning." She stood. "I'd be happy to go with you."

"Where should we go, Grandma?" Emory asked, still glued to her phone.

"Sugar Shoppe on First Avenue is the best candy store, but the Albertson's further down will probably have what you need as well."

Hope saw Enoch stiffen a little at the mention of the candy store, but he didn't say anything so she didn't worry about it. "Sounds like that's where we need to go then," she said, looking to Emory.

"Sounds good. Can you drive, Hope?" Emory asked, still messing with her cell.

Hope huffed a laugh. "I'd better if I don't want us to crash. Using your phone while driving is illegal, you know." She waved to Sheriff Davidson. "And I doubt the sheriff here would be willing to turn a blind eye just because you bribed him with a treat." She smiled when the sheriff chuckled, but Emory just gave her a look.

"Exactly why I asked you to drive. Give me a little credit."

Hope smiled, trying to soothe her cousin's feelings. "Sorry. I was teasing." She headed to the stairs. "Let me grab my stuff and I'll meet you outside."

"Sounds good." Emory continued to mutter to herself as she walked toward the front door.

Hope raced up the stairs and quickly changed her clothes. Running a brush through her hair, she pulled it back in a ponytail and slapped on some lip gloss before grabbing her keys and racing outside. She chuckled when Emory still hadn't looked up from her phone as she leaned against Hope's car. *Guess she wouldn't have noticed if I'd stopped to take a shower.* "What's so interesting?" Hope asked as she unlocked the doors and slid behind the wheel.

"I'm going over plans for my gingerbread house," Emory said, her eyes not moving.

"What? Graham crackers aren't good enough?" Hope joked.

"You do realize this is serious?" Emory stated. "Grandma has won every year for the last ten years. We can't lose now just because they brought in a newbie."

Hope's humor faded as she realized the amount of pressure that Emory must be feeling. "I'm sorry, again. I was just trying to lighten the mood. I wasn't trying to downplay your skills or anything."

Emory sighed and dropped her head against the seat. "No...I'm sorry. I shouldn't have snapped." She groaned. "I'm just so worried that I've shown up to take over and it's all going to be a spectacular failure."

Hope shook her head. "Em, you're amazing. There's a reason why people flock to your baked goods. Because no one makes them quite like you. I'm going to go home fifteen pounds heavier just from being around you this month."

Emory huffed a laugh and turned to look out the window.

"I'm sure that anything you do for the gingerbread village is going to be just as amazing," Hope continued. "You know why?" She glanced at her cousin, then back at the road. "Because *you* made it. Not because you're Claire Simmons' granddaughter, but because you're you."

Emory gave Hope a sad smile. "You always were the cheerleader, you know?" she said.

Hope smiled back. "Someone had to be. Bella was too busy digging up everybody's secrets, and you were too caught up in reading cookbooks."

Emory laughed. "True story." She sighed. "I guess we all ended up doing what we wanted though, huh?"

Hope nodded, but inside she wasn't so sure. They'd all graduated. They all had good credentials, but for some reason, not one of them had a steady job. Though Emory was close. She worked in a hotel kitchen in Seattle, continuing to study and learn under more experienced bakers, but her dream was to open her own storefront, and it was going to take years of saving up her money to make that happen. *Why is life so hard sometimes?* Hope thought. *Although, if we'd all been living good lives, not one of us would have been available to help out Grandma, so I suppose this is a blessing in disguise.*

Determined not to think anymore of it, she pulled to a parking spot on the side of the road in front of Sugar Shoppe and headed inside.

"Hello, welcome to Sugar Shoppe," a perky woman said from the front. Her voice was in direct contrast to her looks. Her hair was dyed midnight black and her makeup overly thick, but her wide smile made her seem friendly enough. "How can I help you today?"

"I've got a list of candies I need for the gingerbread competition," Emory said, stepping forward with her phone open again. "I'm hoping you have everything."

The woman's smile tightened. "I'm sure we do." She studied Hope and Emory. "I'd heard that Claire's granddaughters were coming." She flipped her hair over her shoulder. "I'm Trisha. I was the housekeeper at the Gingerbread Inn before it closed."

Hope swallowed. *Crud. That wasn't who I figured I'd run into our first day in town.* She smiled but didn't reply.

Emory, however, had no such worries. "I'm Emory and this is Hope."

Trisha nodded. "What exactly did you say you needed?"

As Emory began to go down a long list, Hope let her eyes wander around the shop. It really was quite beautiful, in a fun, whimsical sort of way. Bright colors were everywhere. The wall was filled with rainbows as different bulk candies graced the walls. Stands were sprinkled throughout the floor, filled with prepackaged snacks and treats, while a glass counter upfront held fudge and cookies made in house.

"So...I'm assuming you've met Enoch," Trisha ventured as she measured out something Emory had ordered. Trisha's dark brown eyes flitted to Hope, then stayed on Emory. "He's pretty amazing, huh?"

Emory nodded distractedly as she marked something off her list.

Obviously not happy with the response, Trisha turned to Hope. "I've known him since we were kids," she said sweetly. "That man is definitely something...special. I was at his place just last night."

Hope's eyebrows went up, even as her heart plummeted. *He said he was single, and I didn't get the vibe he's a player. So either she's lying or he is, because there's no mistaking her insinuation.* Knowing her grandmother, Hope's instinct said Trisha was pushing the truth, but Hope didn't know for sure. "That's interesting, since he spent most of the evening with us in the house," Hope said, watching closely for the woman's response.

Trisha's smile turned slightly more calculated. "Most isn't all, now is it?"

Hope nodded, conceding the point. She wasn't about to get in a fight with the clerk, nor did Hope know Enoch well enough to stand up for his character. All she could do was wait and see. And guard her heart in the meantime.

ENOCH LOOKED UP FROM where he was working when he heard a car pull into the driveway. He straightened from his wood-working project and watched Hope and Emory get out of the car. They headed to the backseats where each grabbed several bags. Grateful for the excuse to interfere, Enoch rushed out of his work garage and ran to their side.

"Hey!" he called out as he grew closer. "Want some help?"

Hope fumbled a little and turned to look at him. When she smiled, Enoch felt a warm sensation swirl through his chest and he couldn't help but smile back. "Sure," she said easily.

"Let me grab some of those," Enoch said, relieving Hope of half of her burden. "Are there any more in the car?"

"Unfortunately," Hope grumbled with a smile. She looked over her shoulder toward the front door, then back at him and dropped her voice. "I think Emory went a bit overboard, but who am I to tell her no?"

Enoch chuckled. "I'm not sure anyone could tell her no. She seems like a 'do it anyway' type of person."

Hope laughed quietly. "Sort of. I don't think she's a rebel as much as she just doesn't like to back down. If she wants to do it, she's going to do it and that's that." She took in a deep breath. "And right now that includes this gingerbread competition."

Enoch nodded as they began to meander toward the door. "I'll admit it's a pretty big deal. The folks around here look forward to it every Christmas."

"I remember it," Hope said. "But I don't think I realized how big it had grown." She smiled shyly. "When your whole teenage years consist of reading and writing, you don't notice those kinds of things."

Enoch pushed the door with his shoulder and held it open for her. "That's all right. Mine was filled with video games, sawdust and hiding from the world, so I didn't notice it much either," he said with a sheepish smile.

Despite his trying to be funny, Hope frowned. "You know, you said something similar the other night. Why would you feel the need to hide from the world?" she asked, her eyes showed concern. "You were always so nice to us, if a little aloof. I don't understand why you ran out of town after graduation or why you would have stayed away from people."

Enoch shrugged, looking away from her penetrating gaze. There was something about those beautiful, blue eyes that just seemed to see a little deeper. They made him feel vulnerable and it wasn't exactly a sensation he enjoyed. "Isn't every teenage boy that way, a little?" he asked, trying to deflect the question. He didn't share his past with everyone, though many people in the town knew it anyway. His family wasn't exactly a secret. However, here he was, with a woman he would like to impress a little, and stupid stories from his childhood were not how he wanted to start their conversation.

"I suppose so," she murmured. It was clear she didn't quite believe him, but he wasn't ready to spill everything.

Maybe someday, if something developed between us...but not yet. "Should we grab that last batch of bags?" he asked, a wide smile on his face.

Hope groaned as she set her load on the kitchen counter. "I suppose we should." The two of them looked over to see Emory going through the bags and grumbling to herself. "It doesn't look like Emory will be finishing the job."

Enoch took Hope's elbow and guided her toward the door. "That's all right. We've got the manpower to get it done."

She poked his arm. "With biceps like that, I suppose we do." After flexing her own arm, she grimaced. "I'm afraid I don't bring much help with me."

Enoch laughed as they walked back outside. "Don't worry. You be the cheerleader and I'll handle the heavy labor." His smile had turned genuine when she'd teased him about his muscles. Knowing she'd been paying enough attention to him to notice his build was flattering and gave him a bit of courage.

"I can do that," she responded. "I've been told I'm a good cheerleader."

"Then I guess we're the perfect team," Enoch responded.

Her cheeks turned pink and he held back a smirk. "I suppose so," she said softly, tucking a stray piece of hair behind her ear.

"So...did you end up finding what you needed all in one place?" Enoch asked as he loaded his hands with bag handles.

"Um...yep. The Sugar Shoppe had it all." She paused, her smile faltering. "In fact, we even met a friend of yours there."

Enoch winced slightly. "Must be Trisha. She told me she was working there part-time."

Hope gave him a curious look. "That's her." She turned away from him as she closed the car door. "She, uh, hinted that you two were together." Hope's cheeks were so fiery red at this point that Enoch found himself wanting to touch her skin just to see if he could feel the heat.

However, the instance with Trisha stopped him cold. He stopped walking and waited for Hope to stop as well. When he had her full attention, he looked straight into her bright eyes and very seriously said, "Trisha and I are not an item, nor have we ever been one." He sighed. "We went to school together and we're both still here, so we're kind of friends, I guess." He scrunched up his nose. "It's not like there's a ton of choices in a place like Seagull Cove. My guess is she's stuck on me because I'm one of only a few eligible bachelors, not because she actually cares about me."

Hope studied him before nodding sagely at his response. She pinched her lips between her teeth, the lines around her mouth twitching. "Only a few eligible bachelors, huh? Are there ineligible bachelors around here?"

Enoch chuckled as they walked inside. The wind was beginning to pick up and he could tell there would be rain later. "Maybe. Old Man Trundle is eighty if he's a day and has a habit of forgetting his teeth." Enoch set the bags down on the kitchen counter, nodding when Emory muttered a thanks. "I'm not sure most young women like yourself would be interested in someone like him, but," he shrugged, "I've heard of stranger things."

Hope laughed and the redness cleared from her face and neck. "While I'll admit he sounds tempting, he's not exactly what I have in mind."

Enoch rubbed his chin. "I don't know...he's probably got quite the library in that house of his. You might find it to be a dream. You know, kind of a *Beauty and the Beast* situation."

Hope's belly laugh lit Enoch up from the inside out. While she was definitely the quietest of the three cousins, she obviously had a good sense of humor, and the enjoyment on her face only made her all the more beautiful.

She sighed and wiped at the corner of her eye. "That's a good one, thanks."

Enoch grinned. "It was the truth, but you can see my point about Trisha, right?"

Hope sobered a little and studied him. "Yeah. I think I can."

He tilted his head, feeling like there was a little more meaning to her words than he knew, but decided it was a topic for another time. "So, what are you planning to do for the rest of the day?"

Hope put her hands on her hips and looked around the grand foyer they had meandered into. "Well, it occurred to me that no one has volunteered to decorate for Christmas around here, and since I won't be needed at my other job until tomorrow, maybe I should take it on."

A thrum of excitement went through Enoch. "All the decorations are out in the garage. Want some help?" He held his breath. They'd been having a great chat, the air was cleared about Trisha and Enoch was fairly sure that Hope was interested in him as well. *Might as well throw out a lure. The worst that can happen is she'll say no.*

A shy smile crossed her face. "I think I'd like that. Thank you."

CHAPTER 5

"They're in the old servants' garage across the driveway," Enoch said, his smile wide and pleased.

The look of it sent butterflies through Hope's stomach. Not only had this gorgeous guy allayed her fears about Trisha, but he'd also just worked it out so they could spend more time together. What woman in her right mind would turn down such an opportunity? "Let's go, then." She followed him to the door and outside.

Enoch eyed the sky. "It's gonna rain any second, so we better hurry."

Hope wrapped her arms around herself. The temperature had dropped and the wind was whipping around the property. The air felt misty and cold and Hope wanted no part of it.

"Come on." Enoch reached out and grabbed her hand, dragging Hope across the large driveway and into an open garage bay just as the rain began to come down in earnest.

Hope shivered. "Oh my goodness. I should have grabbed a coat this morning."

"I've got a heater in back if you want to come warm up," Enoch offered, waving an arm into the far bay.

"Yes, please." She followed him around tables full of tools and half-done wood projects. As they neared the back, however, she slowed down and her jaw dropped. "Whoa..." Rocking chairs, side tables, carvings and other beautiful artwork were crammed into the space. Each one stunning and obviously made from hand. She ran her hand along the back of a chair, noting how smooth the wood was under her fingertips. "Did you make these?" she asked in awe.

Enoch rubbed the back of his neck and shrugged. "Yeah."

"So this is what you meant when you said the city rid you of your creativity." It was a statement, not a question.

He ticked his head to the side. "Mostly. There's more to it than that, but mostly."

She looked up, meeting his gaze. "I'd love to hear the story sometime."

Enoch smiled sadly. "Someday."

She nodded. After all, she really didn't know him that well. She wanted to, but things were still brand new. Right now, all she was sure of was that she was attracted to him, on both the physical and personality side, and that he seemed to want to get to know her as well. *Guess I'll have to be patient for a bit,* she thought.

"The heater's over here," he said and Hope hurried over at his words.

"Oooh," she groaned, holding out her hands over the electric device. "Heat..."

Enoch chuckled. "It sure helps out here during the cold months, that's for sure."

"So is this where you live?" she asked, looking around. It appeared as if the whole three-car garage was full of his working supplies and Hope began to wonder what he did with all the projects.

"Yep." Enoch pointed up. "I live in the upstairs apartment. I do all the upkeep at the mansion, as well as sell my own stuff online and at summer markets."

She nodded. It made sense. While keeping an old mansion working properly would require plenty of work, he should still have time for other things, such as his woodworking. "I'll bet people pay a mint for things like this," she murmured.

Enoch snorted. "Funny thing is, I sell more stuff to the city people I left behind than I do to anyone else."

Hope grinned. "Sounds about right." She rubbed her hands together. "Okay. Let's grab those decorations and get things going."

"This way, miss," Enoch said formally, making Hope's smile widen.

"Thank you, kind sir," she replied, then headed toward the stairs he indicated. At the top, she opened the door and stepped inside before pausing, waiting for him to join her. In front of her was a studio apartment, which, surprisingly enough, was fairly clean for a bachelor. A few dishes were in the sink, but the bed was made and the floor free of stuff. Beautiful wood furniture dominated the space, from the small dining table, to the matching chairs in front of the picture window and the sleek headboard of the bed.

Hope felt herself blush as Enoch joined her, worried she had been caught gawking at his home. "Um...where to now?" she asked.

Enoch made an exaggerated movement of wiping his brow. "I was a little worried for a second that I'd forgotten to put something away, but it's not as bad as I thought."

Hope laughed lightly. "I have to admit I was just thinking about how clean it was for a single man."

"At least that part of me made a good impression, huh?" he said with a laugh. "Unlike last night."

Hope laughed some more and shook her head. "Last night was just fine," she reassured him. *It was this morning I was worried about. When you saw me with bed-head and in a ratty old sweater.*

"The decorations are in the storage room," he said, turning her around and indicating a door. "One half of the attic was made into an apartment and the other is storage."

"Gotcha." Hope reached for the knob and opened it. "Whew!" She coughed and wiped cobwebs out of her face. "This feels more like Halloween than Christmas."

Enoch stepped up close behind her. "Yeah. It's not usually high on the priority list for the housekeeping staff."

Hope sent him a look over her shoulder. "I'll be sure to tell the new workers what's what."

"Yeah..." Enoch drawled. "She might need a firm hand. Looked a bit like a rebel to me."

Hope laughed quietly. "She sure is." She shivered slightly as Enoch's heat warmed her back. It had been a long time since she'd been so close to a man, and even longer since it was one she was actually interested in. Between grad school, work and her quiet nature, dates weren't quite as plentiful as she would have hoped.

"Let's see here," Enoch said softly.

His breath tickled the back of her neck and Hope found herself stepping backwards slightly. She jumped when he grabbed her shoulders and shifted her to the side so he could walk further into the dark space. *Idiot,* she scolded herself. *All he wanted was to come further inside and you had to go cuddling up to him. What's he going to think now?*

"There we go." Enoch reached above his head and pulled on a chain, which lit the space.

"Much better," Hope agreed, still embarrassed by her faux pas. "But which boxes do we need?" She jumped again when a moaning sound occurred outside, the wind obviously raging.

"These ones," Enoch stated, waving his hand at a tall stack of plastic storage containers. "It'll be a load to take them to the mansion."

Hope whispered under her breath. "And in this weather, no less."

Enoch turned to her. "It sounds like it's pretty nasty outside. Want to grab a cup of hot chocolate and see if we can wait the storm out before we take them over?"

A slow smile crept across Hope's face. "That sounds perfect."

ENOCH MADE SURE HIS sigh of relief was too quiet for Hope to hear. That was twice within the span of a few minutes that he'd gotten bold enough to ask to spend time with her. *Time to put on my game face and go for it.*

He guided her back out into his apartment, shutting the door firmly behind them. Rain slashed against the windows, creating a darker than normal space for as early in the day as it was. "Let me flip on the lights and I'll put some water on." He led her forward, grateful again that he normally kept a fairly tidy home.

Every once in a while, he stayed up late and left his clothes on the floor, and right now that would have been an embarrassing disaster. "If you want to sit on the couch, I'll get things ready." He fumbled through his cupboards, searching for the packets of hot chocolate he usually kept around. When they weren't in their usual space, Enoch felt himself begin to panic. *Calm down. They have to be here somewhere.* He took a fortifying breath. *Geez. You'd think this was my first time with a girl or something.*

"Did you make everything in here?" her soft voice asked, breaking him out of his frustration.

"Uh...yeah," he answered over his shoulder, sending a quick prayer heavenward when he found the mix. Setting it and a packet of cookies on the counter, he turned to look at her. "They were some of the first things I made when I got back."

Her smile was warm and sent liquid heat through his chest. "Looks like you got your creativity back fairly quickly, then."

Enoch shrugged. "Forced it back might have been more like it." His eyes drifted to the window. "Things weren't pretty when I got here, but your grandmother gave me a chance, and it's been the best thing that's ever happened to me."

He looked back to the sitting area to see Hope delicately tracing the design on one of the chairs near the window. The percolator went off behind him and Enoch tore his eyes away from her beauty just long enough to put together a couple of mugs of steaming goodness. Grabbing the package of cookies, he brought it all over to the small table sitting between the chairs. "Have a seat," he offered, waiting until she was settled to hand her the mug. "Careful, it's hot." He almost smacked himself at the mundane comment. *It's HOT chocolate. Of course it's hot. She's gonna think you're an idiot.*

"Mmm..." she hummed. "You buy the good kind." Her smile warmed him up all over again and suddenly the hot chocolate didn't sound as appealing. The back of his neck was sweating to the point where he almost wished he could open a window.

"No point in drinking the bad stuff," he quipped instead. "It's a waste of a good mug."

Hope chuckled. "I like that." She looked out the window while taking a sip. "Kind of an icky storm today, huh?"

Enoch nodded, his eyes still glued to her. There was something very appealing about sitting together quietly chatting. It felt simple. Easy. And suspiciously domestic. He could easily see himself growing attached to moments just like this. *I wonder how set she is on working back in Utah. Would she ever consider something else?*

"How much snow do you guys get here?" she asked, bringing her eyes back to his. "It's been so long since I've come during Christmas that I don't remember."

He shrugged. "Just a few inches here and there. Mostly we're rainy and cold."

Hope nodded and set her mug on the table. "May I?" she asked, reaching for a cookie.

"Help yourself," Enoch encouraged. "That's what they're there for."

Hope smiled as she nibbled. "Well, don't make me eat alone. I'm already freaking out about how much weight I'm going to gain over the holidays, yet I just keep eating."

Enoch quickly shoved a cookie in his mouth, crunching loudly and making Hope laugh. He was beginning to crave that sound. After swallowing he leaned closer. "But just for the record...you're a beautiful woman, Hope. A few pounds here or there isn't going to change that."

Her hand paused on the way to her mouth and a shy smile tugged at her lips. "Why, Enoch Dunlap. I do believe you're flirting with me."

"Are you just now getting that?" Enoch shook his head in feigned disappointment. "I'll have to up my game. It's severely lacking if that's the case."

Hope's smile grew and she turned her face away, but her eyes kept darting back.

Enoch watched her. "Does that bother you?"

She dropped her gaze again, but shook her head. "No. I mean..." Hope set the cookie on the table and brushed off her hands. "It's been longer than I'd like to admit since a man flirted with me, but I can't say I mind." She swallowed hard. "In fact, I might even find myself brave enough to flirt back."

Don't you dare let that go to waste! Enoch shouted at himself. Slowly he stood from his chair and held out a hand to her. "In that case, I think we should get the first awkward thing out of the way."

Hope gave him a smile-frown and took his hand. "What exactly do you mean?" she asked as she stood up.

Stepping a little closer, he put his knuckles under her chin and left a soft kiss on her lips. Despite how short and light the kiss was, Enoch found that his heart was beating faster than a hummingbird's wings and his breathing was definitely shallower than normal. His lips buzzed pleasantly from the sweet touch. He knew it was too fast to give her a real kiss, but something in him was screaming that he needed to make his interest known...and now. "I'm a bit out of practice myself," he whispered, his voice slightly gruff. "I know that was too fast, but I've always found that working the way to the first kiss is the most stressful part of a new relationship."

Hope's eyes were wide, her surprise at his actions clearly evident.

"I mean, if we're both interested in...flirting...we might as well get rid of the awkwardness and look forward to enjoying everything that comes after, right?"

Hope's lips twitched and Enoch felt some of his tension drain that she wasn't running from his apartment and himself. "That is the dumb est reason for a first kiss I have ever heard," she said, laughter in her tone.

He grinned back and shrugged. "It worked, didn't it?"

She pursed those soft pink lips and narrowed her gaze. "I don't know. I could barely feel it to know for sure."

Enoch mentally fist-bumped himself and boldly reached out to wrap his hands around her back. "In that case, maybe I better practice a little. Like I said...it's been a while."

"While I'm also out of practice, I'm afraid of how fast this is," she whispered as his head dropped toward her.

"It is fast," he agreed, letting his lips brush against her cheek. "But I don't think I mind too much...do you?"

"Not as much as I should."

"Do you want me to stop?" Enoch let his hand slide into the hair behind her ear.

"I should...but I don't," she admitted.

"It's just a kiss, right? And you've known me for years...sort of," he whispered against her ear.

She nodded jerkily. Her body language showed how affected she was by his actions and it only spurred Enoch on. "Right," she whispered back. "It's just a little kiss with a boy I've known since I was a teenager." As if her own words were what she needed to hear, Hope turned her head to meet his mouth and the light brush of lips from before became a thing of the past.

Oh, yeah... Enoch thought to himself as he held Claire's beautiful granddaughter in his arms. *I could definitely get used to this.*

CHAPTER 6

Despite the winter weather outside, the next several days felt as if they were full of sunshine and rainbows to Hope. She and Enoch had spent the entire afternoon in his apartment, talking, laughing...kissing...and getting to know each other. It had been fast and frightening, but completely wonderful. And days later, she still found herself touching her lips and smiling.

Every time she and Enoch passed each other on the property, he gave her a secretive smile and would wink at her. It made Hope eager to get up and do her work for the day, just to be able to see him.

In only a few days of being at the Gingerbread Inn, she was finding her heart quickly falling for the handsome handyman who had set her quiet world on fire.

With a grunt, she opened yet another container to find more garland. "How much of this stuff is there?" she muttered, straightening and putting her hands on her hips. She blew out a breath, blowing her bangs out of her face and looking around the front entry. She'd already wrapped garland around the stair rail and over the fireplace. It seemed as if she were running out of places, but obviously it had gone somewhere in the years past.

"Need some help?"

Hope squeaked and jumped when Enoch came up behind her. Spinning around, she scowled and slapped his shoulder. "Don't do that! You scared me half to death."

He laughed and grabbed her hand, holding it against his chest. "You sure?" His knuckle trailed down her hot cheek. "You look alive and well to me."

The flush got deeper at his perusal and Hope had to drop his penetrating gaze. Those sapphire-colored orbs were too much sometimes.

He squeezed her hand. "All joking aside, I really did want to know if you needed help. I've got some free time on my hands."

"If you're up for some more holiday cheer, I could definitely use the help," Hope said in exasperation. She waved her free hand toward the bucket in front of her. "I keep opening more garland, but I have no idea where to put it all."

Enoch chuckled and tucked her into his side, his arm going around her shoulders.

The warmth of his body was luxurious and Hope found herself melting into his embrace.

"I'll try to remember everywhere it was last year." He pursed his lips. "We could always ask Claire, you know."

Hope nodded. "I know, but she's so busy trying to direct Emory's gingerbread work, I'm afraid to interrupt them. They've been planning for days and if it continues, I might start dreaming in gingerbread. It's all they ever talk about."

Enoch laughed again, his chest shaking against her shoulder. "Sounds delicious."

"This stuff isn't," Hope assured him. "They use construction grade gingerbread and it would break a tooth."

"Yeah, but there are always the treats they have around. That baking contest is the dream of every single man ever."

Hope smiled. "Good to know." She glanced up the stairs. "Oh, hello Mrs. Harrison."

A pristinely dressed older woman was walking sedately down the steps. Her dark hair was perfectly coiffed and her pants and shirt pressed to exact angles. "Hello, Hope, dear." She patted her hair as she surveyed all the decorations. "You appear to have a mess on your hands."

Hope plastered a smile on her face. "Yep. I'm trying to figure out how to hang everything just right."

The older woman nodded. "I see. Well, I'm waiting for my son—"

Just as she spoke, a loud knock came on the front door and Hope reluctantly left Enoch's arms to answer it. "Antony," she said with a smile. "You're just in time. Your mother's waiting for you."

Antony Harrison stepped inside and brushed back his chin-length hair. "Hey, Hope. Good to see you again."

Hope had met Antony when he'd dropped off his mother a few days before. She was staying in town for the holidays as Antony lived in Seagull Cove. He had opened a new bakery on the boardwalk last summer and was looking forward to putting his own entry into the gingerbread competition.

His tall, dark looks are enough to win any prize, Hope thought with a chuckle as she closed the door behind him. *But it seems to be sapphires that get my heart racing, instead of stormy clouds.*

"You're late," Mrs. Harrison said with a frown as she came down the last step.

"Looks to me like I'm just on time," Antony said with a grin.

"And you need a haircut," his mother continued.

Hope sighed quietly and went back to Enoch's side, easily slipping her fingers into his.

"Almost makes me miss my mom," he whispered in her ear.

Hope began to chuckle just as stomping could be heard coming down the hallway.

"YOU!" Emory screamed as she reached the front entryway. She marched up to Antony and poked him in the chest. "Where are they?"

Antony gave her a look. "What exactly are you looking for, Emory?" he asked smoothly.

A little too smoothly, thought Hope, though she was also curious as to what Emory was shouting about.

"The candies I brought with me," Emory said through clenched teeth. "The specialty ones I ordered from France." She stepped even closer to Antony. "They're missing."

Antony frowned. "Did you leave them somewhere?"

"Absolutely not!" Emory cried. "I specifically remember bringing them with me."

"And you think my son would have...what?" Mrs. Harrison interrupted. "Stolen them?" She threw up her hands. "What kind of place is this?" she asked. "We come as guests and are accused of being thieves!"

Emory shook her head hard. "I'm not accusing you of anything, Mrs. Harrison. Only your son." She turned back to him. "Only another baker would have known how expensive and special that nougat was. They can only be purchased in France and are specialty items around Christmas."

Antony's eyes were wide. "You have Nougat of Montelimar here? How the heck did you get it?"

"That doesn't matter," Emory said. "Give it back."

Antony put his hands up. "I had nothing to do with it disappearing," he said. "But I'd be happy to help you find it."

"I'm sure you would," Emory snapped.

"Okay..." Hope said, stepping into the hostile situation. "I think maybe we all just need to calm down."

ENOCH DIDN'T LIKE HOPE stepping into the middle of the fight, but he knew there wasn't anything he could do about it. It was like Antony and Emory were going to come to blows with Hope caught between them. *Well, maybe Antony isn't. Emory looks made enough to spit nails at the moment.*

"I am perfectly calm," Antony said with a smirk. "I believe it is your cousin that has gotten her apron in a twist."

Emory growled a little and Hope's eyes widened. "I'm serious, Em. You need to take a step back and calm down."

Emory pinched her lips together and obeyed Hope's orders, but the way she folded her arms over her chest was definitely defensive.

"I don't think we need to stand around and listen to this," Mrs. Harrison sniffed. "This...woman...obviously has issues. We should just—"

"Not so fast, Mother," Antony inserted. "I want to hear what Emory has to say." He folded his arms in return. "After all, she's convinced I'm the cause of her distress and I, for one, would like to know why."

Emory shook her head hard as Hope stepped back a little. Once she was within range, Enoch grabbed her hand and tugged her into his side. He felt better immediately, knowing she was close enough for him to protect if something got crazy.

"I brought some candies and desserts with me for the Christmas party and gingerbread competition. They were expensive, specialty treats and now one of the best ones is missing." She turned to Hope mid-explanation. "Most people would never know how hard it is to get that nougat. Only another baker," she shot a glare at Antony, "would know. Not to mention he's looking to win this year in order to further his career."

"So you think Antony what? Came in in the middle of the night and stole it?" Hope asked. "Emory, that's a pretty bold accusation."

"Hear, hear," Antony echoed. "First of all, there is no honor in winning by ruining someone else." He raised an eyebrow at Emory. "Secondly, why would I bother to sneak in in the middle of the night?" he asked cooly, stepping closer to Emory.

Enoch's eyebrows shot up. He had to give it to the guy. He was gutsy. *So gutsy it might end with him decapitated.*

"When I know that you would let me in at any time, hm?"

"You arrogant—"

"What exactly is going on here?"

The entire group spun to see Bella with her hands on her hips and her foot tapping.

"There's a story here. I can smell it and somebody better tell it to me."

Hope pinched the bridge of her nose. "Not now, Bella."

"Yes, now." Bella marched up to the group. "As loud as you all are, we're going to start getting complaints and I'm going to have to deal with it. Count this as me being preemptive."

"Emory's foreign candy is missing and she's accusing Antony," Enoch said with a sigh. He shrugged when Hope looked at him incredulously. "What? Did you really think you would keep it from her? She's got a nose like a bloodhound."

Bella preened under the words. "Why, thank you."

Hope shook her head and turned back to Emory. "Em, unless you have some proof that Antony did something, then we need to back down. Do you have proof?"

For the first time during that fight, Emory deflated. "No," she said flatly. "But I'm meticulous in how I organize my things. Nothing of mine ever goes missing." She stared hard at Hope. "Ever. The nougat is gone. Which means someone took it."

"Okay." Hope nodded her head. "Why don't you, me and Bella go do a search for it, just to see if someone misplaced it. If that doesn't work, we'll focus on what to do next."

Enoch's heart fell. He'd been looking for some alone time with Hope. Something they hadn't had since their kiss a few days ago. They'd crossed paths, but both had been working and unable to take more than a few minutes for a break. Helping her finish the decorating was supposed to give him a chance to be at her side and maybe ask her out for an actual date.

"Fine," Emory snapped, her eyes darting to Antony and back to Hope. "But no one else is allowed in my kitchen except you two."

"About time you saw sense," Mrs. Harrison said. She walked to the front door. "Antony, we're late. We need to leave."

He reached around his mother to grasp the door handle, then paused to look at Emory. "You'll let me know when you find it?" he asked.

"Why do you care?" Emory shot back.

"Because believe it or not, I'm not the bad guy you make me out to be," Antony said, turning his body to face her fully.

Their eyes met and Enoch could feel the tension in the room turn up a notch. *Those two might not hate each other as much as they pretend,* he mused.

After a moment, however, Antony broke the seriousness with a cocky smirk. "After all, who can be a bad guy with this kind of hair?" He pushed a hand through his dark locks, seeming to enjoy the reaction he was getting from the other baker.

"Antony," his mother said with a tsk of her tongue while Emory gasped in outrage. To her credit, Hope groaned, but Bella laughed out loud. "You must stop this now." Mrs. Harrison pulled open the door and grabbed his arm. "Enough of this tomfoolery. We go."

Enoch watched them leave, feeling slightly lost at the situation. It had all happened so fast and the emotions were practically choking him. He found himself stepping backward, Hope's hand still in his.

"Where are you going?" Bella asked pointedly.

Enoch froze and Hope looked at him before laughing softly.

"I think he's been scarred," Bella teased, crossing her arms over her chest.

"I just want my nougat," Emory said. Her shoulders were rounded and she was rubbing her temples. "Someone had to have stolen it. There's no other explanation."

Hope opened her mouth, but Bella beat her to the punch. Wrapping her arm around her cousin, Bella began to lead Emory out of the foyer. "Let's look together," she said encouragingly. "According to scaredy-cat Enoch over there, I can sniff out anything. I'm sure nougat won't be a problem at all." She grinned over her shoulder and sent Enoch and Hope a wink.

Hope relaxed back into Enoch's chest. "Oh good," she whispered. "I wasn't looking forward to searching for something as nasty as nougat."

Enoch chuckled, causing Hope to bounce a little. "Not a fan? It sounded like this stuff was pretty special."

"French nougat is still nougat," Hope said with a dramatic shiver.

"You don't like it at all?"

She shook her head and peered at him over her shoulder. "Nope. I can't even eat a Snickers because of that layer." Hope scrunched up her nose. "Gross."

Enoch let go of her hand and wrapped his arms around her from behind. "So noted. No boxes of nougat and roses."

Hope smiled. "Roses are fine. Nougat is garbage."

He laughed. "Got it." Enoch looked around at the decorating mess still sitting around them. "Should we get on that garland now? It looks like we've been left to our task."

"Perfect," Hope said, stepping out of his embrace. "Let's get to it."

CHAPTER 7

"You know..." Hope mused from her place at the bottom of the ladder. "It's funny that Emory said someone stole her stuff."

"Why is that funny?" Enoch asked as he hung decorations from the chandelier.

"Well, I'd forgotten about it, but yesterday a bottle of hand soap was missing from my supply closet."

Enoch frowned and paused his work. Resting one arm across the top of the ladder, he looked down. "Like...a whole bottle?"

Hope pursed her lips and nodded. "Yeah. I don't know if you know this, but Grandma doesn't like to use refillable stuff. She buys the fancy, really good-smelling soaps. All the extras are lined up nice and neat in the supply closet, and yesterday when I went to grab one, I noticed one was gone." She shrugged, her mind spinning. "I didn't think much of it at the time. I mean...it's soap. Somebody obviously just needed it." She peered back up at Enoch, who was listening intently. "But with the missing candy, it makes me wonder if there's something more to it."

Enoch scratched his chin. "Huh. Kind of sounds suspicious, but what exactly does it mean? Is one of the guests a thief? It's all older couples checked in right now." He shook his head. "It just doesn't seem very plausible."

"I totally agree," Hope stated. "But doesn't that seem weird? For two things to go missing back to back?"

Enoch went back to work and was quiet for a few seconds. "I guess so. But they might both have easy explanations as well."

"Like what?"

"Like maybe one of your cousins needed soap," he explained. "Or maybe Emory forgot the candy back home. Or misplaced it here. Or someone else moved it from the spot she designated."

"I suppose you're right," Hope said, handing another string of lights up to him.

Enoch chuckled. "You sound disappointed."

Hope's head shot up. "No way. I came here looking to help Grandma and take a break from running myself ragged. I certainly didn't come to solve a mystery." She grinned. "That's Bella's department."

"And Bella is on the case!" Bella shouted as she waltzed into the foyer, studying their work. "Coming along nicely, guys. Good job."

"What do you mean, you're on the case?" Hope asked with a frown. "There isn't a case."

Bella pumped her eyebrows. "There is now."

Enoch climbed down the ladder and stood beside Hope. She leaned into him a little. His presence and warmth were wonderful, and she couldn't seem to get enough.

"Care to explain further?" he asked, disapproval in his voice.

Bella clasped her hands behind her back and leaned in conspiratorially. "We found the nougat."

Hope looked to Enoch, then back to Bella. "Then why is there a case?"

One side of Bella's mouth curled into a satisfied smirk. "Because the nougat was gone. We only found the wrapper."

Hope's jaw dropped. "Someone ate her candy? So we really do have a thief?" Enoch's strong arm came around her shoulders, grounding her sudden worries. The idea of someone sneaking around taking things was unnerving. Hope wasn't the kind of person who sought out adventure. She preferred to leave that to her books.

"It appears that way," Bella said, rocking back on her heels. "Either that, or someone got *really* hungry in the middle of the night and thought the kitchen was fair game."

"Maybe we need to talk to the guests," Enoch suggested. "Make sure that wasn't what actually happened."

"Oh, I plan to," Bella assured them. "I'm totally going to get to the bottom of this."

A little shiver ran up Hope's spine and Enoch rubbed her back. "Go for it. I don't want to be involved."

"Chicken," Bella teased.

"Better a chicken than getting involved in something with a criminal," Hope shot back.

"No one has to get *involved*," Bella said with an eye roll. "You make it sound so...clandestine. I said I was going to catch them, not kiss them."

Hope shook her head. "It's all yours."

Bella rubbed her hands together. "Awesome." She spun on her heel and began walking back toward the front desk. "But where to start?" she muttered. "I wonder if someone could lift fingerprints from the wrapper..."

Enoch chuckled. "She's certainly gung-ho about it, isn't she?"

Hope sighed. "Yeah. And it'll be me who ends up saving her from going too far." She looked at Enoch. "Sometimes I don't know how we're related. She got all the courage and I got all the fear, but it usually takes the two of us to even each other out."

Enoch used his hand on her back to turn her toward him, then wrapped his other hand around her waist. "Don't worry," he said, leaving a light kiss on her forehead. "I'm perfectly content with you being a chicken."

"Hey!" Hope cried out, feigning anger. She slapped his chest, but he only laughed and pulled her in for a hug.

"Hope?"

"Hmm?" she asked as she snuggled into his chest.

"Would you go on a date with me?"

Hope straightened and looked him in the eye. "We kind of did things backward, didn't we?"

Enoch shrugged. "I don't really mind. I mean, I didn't exactly plan to hit step number two first, but I'm not complaining either."

Hope smiled, excitement fluttering through her chest. "I'm not complaining either, and I would love to go out with you."

Enoch's joy-filled smile was nearly blinding. The happiness on his face was contagious and Hope found her own grin growing wider. He brought their foreheads together. "As excited as I am for that," he said, his voice soft, "I do find I have one thing to complain about."

"What's that?" Hope asked, closing her eyes to better feel the sensations running through her at his touch and nearness.

"That we haven't had enough time to repeat our time in my apartment," he said against her cheek.

Hope's heart skipped a beat as she imagined another wonderful kiss from this handsome man. She opened her eyes and made a point of looking around. "I don't see anyone stopping us," she replied.

Enoch stepped back, making her frown, but then held out his hand. "Come with me," he said.

Feeling giddy, Hope slid her hand into his and followed him down the hall and into the laundry room. Once inside, he closed the door and immediately drew her close.

"You have too many cousins around to kiss you properly in the front entryway," he said huskily.

"So you thought the laundry room would be a better place?" she teased, looking at the dryer, which was currently tumbling a batch of towels.

"It's perfect," he explained, kissing her jawline. Then he straightened and pulled something out of his pocket. Hope laughed when she recognized the little plant with red berries. "And no one will interrupt us," Enoch said with a pump of his eyebrows.

As her skin heated up from his suggestion, Hope found herself eager for more and threw her arms around his neck. "Sounds good to me," she whispered, then pulled his mouth to hers.

ENOCH CHUCKLED AT HER enthusiasm before taking the situation more seriously. With them both working, who knew how long it would be before he could get her alone again?

Just as he was getting lost in the feel of her, the door opened, then quickly slammed shut again, causing Hope to jerk away.

"Oh my word," she whispered, smoothing her hair. "I hope that wasn't Grandma."

Enoch shook his head and helped her with her hair. "Nah. She wouldn't have stepped back out. She would have stayed and teased us." He cleared his throat as he noticed her bright red lips, which were slightly swollen from his attention. Seeing them only made him want more, but he held himself in check. Someone was obviously needing to get into the room. "Give me a second," he said, walking to the door and opening it.

He frowned and pulled the door open wider. "Hello?" Enoch looked both ways down the hall, but there was no one there.

"Who was it?" Hope asked, coming up beside him.

"I have no idea," Enoch said, an eerie feeling crawling across his shoulders. "No one was there."

"Good grief, this really is feeling more like Halloween than Christmas anymore," Hope whispered, holding onto his arm. "What the heck is going on?"

Enoch shook his head. "I don't know, but maybe we should follow Bella's example and try to get to the bottom of it."

Hope scrunched up her nose. "She wasn't kidding when she said I was a chicken. I don't go looking for adventure...ever."

"Maybe so, but this time you'll be with me, so it'll be all right," Enoch encouraged.

Hope sighed. "Why do I have the feeling I'm going to regret this?" she muttered.

Enoch huffed a laugh. "Because you probably are." He wrapped his arm around her shoulders and led her out of the room. "We'd better get those decorations done before someone trips on them and your grandma gets sued."

"Good idea," Hope said, hurrying her steps. "I'm not very good at my job, am I?"

Enoch kept pace with her and they arrived back at the sitting room quickly. "You're great at your job. But your job isn't being an interior decorator. That's just something you're doing on the side."

Hope smiled gratefully at him. "Thanks."

He winked before picking up the ladder and moving it to the next place. "Anytime."

They worked in relative silence for the next hour as they slowly moved around the house putting up all the decorations.

"I can't believe Grandma has this done every year," Hope panted as she stretched to reach a high shelf. "It was always magical when I was a kid, but I never stopped to think about how much work it would be."

"I doubt any kid does," Enoch agreed. "And yeah. I've helped out while I've been here and it's always a crazy amount of work." He grinned at her from his place across the room. "But the guests love it and it's always worth it to see the little kids' eyes light up."

"I have to admit I'm excited for us to do the tree," Hope said with a smile. "I wanted to do it last. Because it always seems to be the crowning glory, ya know?"

Enoch nodded. "Gotcha." He chewed his lip. "Does Emory know that Claire does fresh gingerbread cookies for the tree every year?"

Hope groaned. "Oh my gosh, no. Don't tell her. She's already stressed to the hilt." Hope glanced toward the doorway, then back. "She feels like she has to prove something in all this." Hope waved her arms around. "Like Grandma is going to hold her to some kind of crazy standard since she went to culinary school and everything."

"That doesn't sound fun."

Hope nodded. "It isn't. She could hardly bring herself to look away from her phone when we went to the candy store the other day. And I don't think she's talked about anything but business since she got here."

"That and thieving bakers," Enoch snorted.

Hope covered her mouth to hide her laughter, but it bubbled out anyway. "So true!"

Enoch laughed with her.

"Actually, all the stress is probably why she snapped at him. She's wound too tight at the moment," Hope stated, her voice growing sad. "I was hoping our time together here would be relaxing. We haven't been together as cousins or with Grandma in ages." She sighed. "But now it seems like that's not going to be the case."

Enoch squished his lips to the side. "Yeah...life doesn't always turn out the way we want, that's for sure."

"Good thing I met a handsome handyman who asked me out," Hope teased, going back to decorating. "It's made things a bit cheerier around here."

Enoch chuckled. "I find myself grateful for that as well."

Hope laughed out loud and they went back to their work. It wasn't long before they were joined by others, however.

"Oh, Hope..." Grandma Claire said, clasping her hands beneath her chin. "It's just beautiful, honey!"

"Thanks, Grandma," Hope said, walking over to give her a kiss. "Here. Let me help you to a chair."

"On it," Enoch interrupted, rushing over to put his arm around Claire. Hope stepped back and sent him a grateful smile, and Enoch felt his chest puff up just a little. He helped Claire sit down and smiled when she patted his cheek.

"You do wonderful work, dear," Claire said. "How do you enjoy having a beautiful woman to do it with?" she asked with a wink.

"Grandma!" Hope gasped.

Enoch laughed. "It makes everything better," he answered.

Claire nodded firmly. "That's as it should be."

"What's as it should be?" Bella asked, coming in with purpose in her steps. She held her phone between her hands and was typing furiously.

"Nothing," Hope quickly answered, then gave Enoch a look when he dared to open his mouth.

He snapped his jaw shut, but pumped his eyebrows at her, bringing that blush that he enjoyed to her cheeks.

"When are you going to man up and ask her out?" Bella asked as she plopped herself on the couch, still typing.

"Oh my word!" Hope cried. "What is wrong with all of you?"

"What?" Bella asked. "By the way you've been swooning all week and touching your lips, he has to have kissed you, but you haven't gone out on a date. I just want to make sure he's doing it right."

"For your information," Enoch said calmly, while Hope gasped for air, "I did ask her out. Now I just need to plan it."

"Good man," Bella said with a smile as Claire offered her congratulations as well. She turned to Hope. "Just make sure you don't accuse him of stealing your nougat, and you might have a shot."

CHAPTER 8

As Hope padded down the steps the next morning, she wrapped her arms around herself and shivered. "Man, it's cold." Her heavy sweatshirt seemed to be doing nothing in the cool morning air. "I wonder if there's a problem with the heater."

She stood in the foyer, noting it was even colder there than on the stairs. When a stray piece of hair floated around her face, Hope turned toward the breeze. It seemed to be coming from the hallway that led to all the utility areas. She leaned around the corner and squeaked. An outside door at the end of the hallway was wide open and an icy breeze straight off the ocean was filling the house.

Hope looked around, noting she was alone, then rushed down the hall and locked the door. Once done, she leaned against it and caught her breath. "Who would leave that open?" she mused.

"Hope?"

She looked up and gave a weak wave to Emory.

"What's going on?"

Hope pushed off the door and shook her head. "I don't know. It was freezing when I got downstairs this morning. I just discovered the door was open."

Emory frowned and looked beyond Hope to the offending exit. "That's weird. No one uses that door that I know of. It leads to the side of the house with the gardener's shed. Who would go that way this time of year?"

Hope shrugged. "I have no idea. All I know is it's cold and when people start waking up, they aren't going to like it."

"Neither are my pastries," Emory grumbled, turning and hurrying back the way she came. "Good thing we have a while before they get up."

Hope took a deep breath and felt her muscles relax as she entered the hot kitchen. The stove and oven were both running, helping heat the space, though it was noticeably cooler than usual. "I think I'm gonna go light a fire in the grand hall," she said, walking toward the door to that room. "It should help get rid of the chill."

"Good idea," Emory said, her attention back on her food.

Hope crumpled up some paper and put it in the hearth before stacking the logs above it in a teepee style, just like Grandpa had taught her when she was a young girl. Grabbing the lighter, she started the edge of the crumpled news and paused to watch the flame eat the paper. She was so caught up in the intoxicating display that she didn't hear anyone come in behind her.

"Is the heater broken?" Enoch's deep voice asked, slightly raspy from the early hour.

"Oh!" Hope spun and fell onto her backside at the surprise. "Good grief, you startled me," she scolded, scrambling to her feet in embarrassment. She tucked her hair behind her ears, grateful she'd made herself at least semi-presentable before coming downstairs.

Enoch was smiling as he watched her get herself together, looking completely unrepentant that he'd snuck up on her.

"And no," she said a little more forcefully than necessary. "The heater's fine...at least as far as I know."

The fire caught onto the logs and burst to life behind her, catching Hope's attention. She shifted, letting the sudden heat penetrate her jeans and legs.

Enoch frowned.

"I found the door that leads to the south side of the house wide open this morning." Hope rubbed her upper arms. "I have no idea how long it had been that way, but the foyer was icy."

"Still is," Enoch said, stepping further into the room. "I wonder what happened."

Hope's head shot up. "You don't think it had anything to do with our thief, do you?"

Enoch rubbed his chin. "Is anything else missing?"

Hope pinched her lips between her teeth as she thought. "Not that Emory mentioned, and she's the only one I've seen this morning."

He took a deep breath as he stepped up beside her. "Well...unless something is missing, it might just be that someone walked out and didn't close it all the way."

"But why would anyone be going that direction?" Hope asked. "Surely none of the guests would be going out a utility door, and none of us would have a reason to go to the garden shed, at least not at this time of year."

Enoch nodded. "I agree, but it's the only thing it can be." He grinned. "It's not like the mansion is haunted or anything."

Hope rolled her eyes. "First thieves and now ghosts. If I didn't know any better, I'd say you were trying to run us out of town."

Enoch chuckled and wrapped his arms around her waist. "Good thing you know better, then." Leaning down, he gave her a soft, short kiss. "Good morning," he whispered, looking deeply into her eyes.

Hope's shivers changed to something far more pleasurable as she rested her hands against his chest. "Good morning," she answered back. His strong, warm presence certainly changed the way the house had felt only moments earlier.

"I was hoping you might be free tonight to go on that date we talked about," Enoch hedged.

"I should finish the housecleaning by early afternoon," Hope said softly, letting her fingers play with the hair on the back of his head. "So this evening is definitely free." She tilted her head to the side. "Unless we have another phantom issue, that is."

Enoch kissed the end of her nose. "No phantoms. Got it."

He let her go just as Emory came back in. "You going to help out or keep kissing all day?" she asked, raising her eyebrows.

Hope shook her head, embarrassed at being caught, but knowing that Emory wasn't trying to be cruel. She just said it like it was. "I'm coming."

"Me too," Enoch quickly said. "What do you need?"

"The table needs to be set and the buffet put out," Emory rattled off as they went back to the kitchen area. Smells of cinnamon and sugar wafted through the space along with the salty smell of bacon and eggs, creating a smorgasbord for the senses.

Hope paused to take a deep whiff. She loved that smell. It had been missing in her tiny apartment. The hot plate she used wasn't much help in making baked goods. *While I managed to get through school with no loans, sometimes it doesn't feel like much of a win.* While she wasn't paying for tuition anymore, she was definitely at the bottom of the barrel. Without a full-time income, she was still living like the poor college student she had hoped to leave behind.

But I'm not starving and I have access to all the sweets I want at the moment. That'll have to be enough. Her eyes trailed over Enoch's sturdy frame. *And I've got a date with the most handsome man at the mansion. Yeah...I think life is pretty good.*

ENOCH FOUND HIMSELF not just excited for his first official date with Hope, but his mind had been spinning all day with worry. It all just seemed too...something. The eaten candy. The open door. The stolen soap. Not to mention the way his tools had been shifted around and the weird accident that led to Claire's surgery. How was it related? Or was it related? Were they really what they looked like at face value or was there something deeper simmering just under the surface?

Enoch wasn't one to panic, but he found himself more anxious than normal and the answer to why was standing before him in a stunning knee-length dress with her hair spilling across her shoulder in very tempting curls. The light blue of the dress was the perfect complement to make her eyes pop and gave her blonde hair an eye-catching backdrop.

"Wow..." he croaked. Clearing his throat, he grinned sheepishly and rubbed the back of his neck. "You look ethereal."

Hope's eyes dropped to the floor, but she was smiling widely. "Thank you," she answered shyly.

His black dress shirt and blue jeans didn't seem quite enough standing next to the beauty beside him, but changing his clothes wasn't an option at this point, so he pressed forward. "Ready, then?"

Hope peeked up from under her lashes and nodded. "Yep."

"Great." Feeling like he needed to be extra formal, Enoch turned around and offered her his arm. He preferred to hold her hand, but there was just something about the way she looked that demanded him to be a little more gentlemanly.

"Don't forget a coat!" Claire called out from the entrance to the grand ballroom.

Enoch and Hope both looked that way to see Bella and Emory standing with their grandmother. Both the cousins were grinning widely.

"Aw...my baby cousin is all grown up and kissing boys!" Bella teased, wiping a fake tear from her eye.

"Oh my gosh," Hope whispered. "We better get out of here before they say anything else."

Enoch couldn't stop his smile, but he managed to swallow the laughter. Even though Bella was more outspoken than he was attracted to, Enoch couldn't help but find her remarks humorous. She was definitely the jokester of the group. Emory, on the other hand, didn't laugh as much, but she was more intuitive about others' feelings than Bella was.

Hope tugged on his sleeve. "Come on," she said, walking toward the door.

She had put on her coat while Enoch had been holding in his laughter and he felt a small surge of shame that he hadn't helped her with it. "On it," he said, coming back to the present.

"Don't do anything I wouldn't do!" Bella called out and Claire cackled at the words, but Emory wasn't as impressed.

"They're not going to be hunting criminals," she snapped.

"I never said they were," Bella retorted.

"Nor is she going to annoy him to death with questions—" Emory's scolding was cut off when Hope pulled the front door closed behind them.

"Wow...that was embarrassing." She groaned.

Enoch let his laughter out and took her hand, leading her to his SUV. "They're funny," he reassured her. "It must be nice to have family who loves you."

Hope gave him a look and Enoch wanted to smack himself. "I'd still like to hear that story," she said softly as she climbed into the passenger seat.

Enoch sobered and nodded. "Well...tonight might be your lucky night." After seeing her settled, he went to the driver's side and backed them out of the driveway. They were quiet for the first few moments, but Enoch found it wasn't uncomfortable. In fact, nothing with Hope was uncomfortable. He enjoyed her smile and laugh, but also just enjoyed her. She was peaceful, helpful, kind and made him feel good about himself, and none of those things had to do with how stunning she was.

The more his mind pondered, the more he realized he was starting to lose his heart to this soon-to-be teacher. *But what exactly to do about it?* he thought. *It's too fast for anything right now. I suppose the right thing to do would be to just keep going. Only time will tell if it all turns out.*

"I hope seafood is okay," he said, glancing her way.

"I love shrimp," she gushed, making Enoch smile.

"Good. I figured it might be nice on a cold day like today." He leaned over slightly. "Not to mention it's the nicest place in town, unless you want bar food."

Hope grinned. "I like a greasy bite too, but fish is perfect."

Enoch nodded, then switched hands on the steering wheel and reached over to grab hers. He rested their combined digits on his thigh while he drove. "So...any idea where you'll end up teaching?" he asked, hoping he sounded nonchalant.

Hope twisted her lips around. "No. There haven't been any full-time openings where I'm at, which is why I keep subbing." She sighed. "But I'm sure if I was willing to move, I could find something."

Enoch swallowed hard. "You don't want to move?"

She ticked her head back and forth. "I don't know. For the right situation I would, I guess. But I like the city I'm in. I like the amenities." A short, harsh laugh came from her. "Not that I can afford any of them right now, but I'd like to someday."

His heart fell a little. Seagull Cove was definitely small and it sounded like she wouldn't even consider a place like this. "I see."

Hope squeezed his hand. "Truth be told, I'd move just about anywhere if the situation called for it," she said softly.

He wasn't sure if she was trying to make him feel better or just saying things, so he let it go, but his enthusiasm had died down a bit. *I guess I could follow her if we got to that point, but it would be hard to leave Claire. Especially since I finally feel like I've found where I belong.* "Here we are," he said with forced cheer, pulling into the parking lot.

Hope was frowning a little when he came around to her door. "Did I say something wrong?" she asked, her voice showing her worry.

Enoch shook his head and shoved the too-early concerns away. "Nope." He smiled, soaking in her beauty once more. "Everything is just right."

CHAPTER 9

Something felt off to Hope as they were seated at their table. She wasn't sure what had happened, but somewhere during the short ride to the restaurant, she'd said something Enoch didn't like. The idea that she had somehow hurt him or made him upset caused a physical ache in her chest, and she had to fight the urge to rub the spot.

But what did I say?

"Trisha?"

Enoch's question brought Hope out of her mental wanderings.

What? The candy shop girl?

Hope twisted in her seat to see where Enoch was looking.

"Hey, Enoch," Trisha said with a wide smile. Her dark lipstick showed off her white teeth. Sashaying her hips, Trisha walked toward their table and Hope was able to see that the woman's make up was just as dark as her lip stain. Thick eyeliner and eyeshadow created a slightly goth vibe and the black lacy dress only reiterated the style choice. "Fancy meeting you here."

Hope felt her cheeks go hot when Trisha pointedly ignored her.

Enoch leaned back in his chair. "I didn't realize you were dating someone," he said with a smile. "Do I get to meet him?"

Trisha gave a husky laugh. "I'm sure that can be arranged." Still ignoring Hope, Trisha slid into one of the extra seats at their table. "Have you tried the salmon here? It's to die for."

Enoch gave an awkward laugh and looked at Hope. She gave him a small smile, hoping it hid her irritation.

"Um...Trisha, have you met Hope?" Enoch asked, reaching across the table for her hand.

Hope smiled, ignoring the look of fury in Trisha's eyes.

"We have," Trisha said with fake sweetness. "She came into the candy store." She paused. "You and your...cousins are still around? I would have thought you finished helping your grandma by now."

Hope opened her mouth, then snapped it shut. *Wow...what's her deal? I mean, she obviously likes Enoch, but he's here with me...holding MY hand. Can't she take a hint?*

"They're here until after the new year," Enoch hurried to say.

"Huh," Trisha huffed. "Looks like Christmas wishes do come true."

Hope's eyebrows shot up. "Excuse me?"

Trisha smiled and stood from her seat. "I can tell I'm intruding," she said, again with the sickeningly sweet tone.

"And I'm sure your date is wondering where you are," Hope added firmly. She didn't like confrontation. Not at all, but this woman was out of bounds.

Trisha's eyes narrowed. "Right." She turned to Enoch. "I'll be seeing you." Once again her eyes turned to daggers when they met Hope's, then the woman flounced off, throwing her black hair over her shoulder.

"That was...awkward...and weird. Definitely weird," Enoch stammered. He turned to Hope, clasping her hand between both of his. "I'm really sorry. I had no idea she would be here."

Hope shook it off. "No worries. I know you didn't." She huffed a laugh. "But she doesn't seem to take a hint, does she?"

Enoch shook his head. "Not really. But wow...that was way bolder than I've ever seen her before." He closed his eyes and shook his head again. "I'm really sorry. I just...I don't really know what to say."

Hope smiled. "Then let's forget it happened, okay? I have to admit I'm feeling pretty selfish, because I'm not really that sorry that she's not getting what she wants."

A single brow slowly rose up. "Oh? And why is that?"

Still feeling slightly worried from his reaction in the car, she smiled hopefully at him. "Because I'm hoping it means that I'm getting what I want instead."

Enoch's face softened and his eyes roamed over her. "If you're getting what you want, then that makes two of us. I've never been interested in Trisha. And even if you weren't here, that wouldn't change."

"Good to know." Hope let go of his hands and picked her menu back up. "So...what's good here?" She glanced up. "Anything but the salmon."

He chuckled and looked at his own menu. "I'm a fan of the capellini and the wood grilled shrimp. Really, you can't go wrong with anything here."

"Perfect," Hope said.

After the waiter had taken their orders, Hope decided it was time to push Enoch for a little more. She folded her hands in her lap. "So...how about that story now?"

Enoch pinched his lips together. "Are you sure you want to know? Not all stories have happy endings."

Anxiety arose within her and Hope worried she'd gone too far. "You don't have to tell me anything," she reassured him softly. "I just wanted to get to know you better, know where you came from and all that jazz." She shook her head. "But you don't have to tell me."

Enoch sighed. "Fair is fair," he stated, leaning back. "You told me about you, I suppose it's my turn." One side of his mouth pulled up into a sarcastic grin. "I know we knew each other a bit when we were younger, but since you were only around at Christmas and a few years behind me, you probably had no idea that I was a bit on the cocky side."

Hope jerked back a little. "Really? I wouldn't call you that. Antony maybe, but not you."

Enoch laughed and nodded. "Antony is a good guy, but yeah...he's got an ego on him."

Hope smiled, but it felt shaky. She was growing more concerned for him by the second.

"And maybe cocky isn't the right word. I was...angry. Really angry. Life had been hard and I wanted out." Enoch turned his face and looked out the window. "I'm not sure how I planned to do that, especially since I was just a woodworker, but I just knew that if I took my stuff to somewhere bigger than Seagull Cove that life would turn into roses rather than thorns."

Hope whistled low. "Big plans."

"Yeah, well...I had to find something to push me forward, since I definitely wasn't staying here." He blew out a breath and rested his arms on the table, playing with his water glass. "My dad was the town drunk and if I knew anything, it was that if I didn't get out then, I probably wouldn't get out at all. My mother was gone by the time I was fourteen, so it was just me and the old man."

Hope gasped, compassion and sympathy flooding her as she thought of what it must have been like to grow up with a parent like that. *No wonder he enjoys my family so much. We tease all the time, but we all love each other. Oh my gosh, it all makes sense now.*

"I REALLY DON'T THINK we need to go into details," Enoch forced himself to continue. "Suffice it to say that I didn't leave my father on good terms. And yet life in the city seemed to suck out my very soul." He shook his head. "It was too loud, too busy and just too...impersonal." *And that's where Hope wants to live. Would I be willing to do that if she was with me?*

"No wonder you clammed up when I talked about living in one," Hope murmured.

Enoch made a face. "Sorry. I wasn't trying to rain on your parade. I guess we all have our own opinions about places like that."

Hope nodded. "True. But I'd like to hear about you coming back home...if that's all right?"

Enoch nodded, knowing he should finish the story. After all, Hope's grandmother had a large part in it. "After realizing wood-style furniture wouldn't make much of a splash in a contemporary setting, I packed up and came back home." He took in a deep breath. "I didn't have much to my name, and hoped Dad would forgive me enough to let me stay with him until I got back on my feet." Enoch slowly shook his head. "No such luck. He saw it was me on the doorstep and slammed the door in my face."

Hope gasped and their conversation quickly shut down when the waiter brought their food.

Enoch let them eat for a moment before finishing. "Long story short, your grandmother saw me camped out on the street corner and took me home." He laughed harshly. "It sounds like I was a stray dog, now that I think of it."

"I'm sure that's not how she saw it," Hope reassured him.

Enoch nodded. "I know. She offered me work in exchange for room and board, and we set off from there. Over the past couple of years, she's become like family. She allowed me to take over the whole garage so I could still have my creative outlet. I've discovered a whole new market online and can make a decent income with my hobby while still working full-time for your grandma." He took a large bite of pasta and chewed for a minute. "And then you came back and my world was taken for a spin."

He loved the pink that rose to her cheeks at his words.

"Flatterer."

Enoch grinned. "Just callin' it like I see it."

She laughed lightly and shook her head. "If we're both being truthful, then I'll admit I didn't expect to be asked out by a handsome woodworker. I was planning on some peace, quiet and good food." She smiled. "I don't think anything has been quiet since I arrived."

Enoch pursed his lips and nodded. "Yeah...you and your cousins have shaken things up, that's for sure."

Hope laughed quietly. "I hope it hasn't all been bad."

He bumped his foot against hers under the table. "It hasn't been bad at all."

An hour later Enoch pulled back into the driveway at the mansion. He shut off the engine, but didn't move. "Is it too bold to tell you that I'm not ready to let you go yet?"

He couldn't see the exact color of her cheeks in the darkness, but the pleased smile crossing her lips told him they were probably bright pink. "Am I too bold if I admit I feel the same way?"

"We really are the perfect pair," he said, slipping out of the vehicle to open her door. He took her hand and began to guide her to his apartment. "Wanna grab some popcorn or cocoa and watch a movie?"

Hope ducked into his shoulder as a cold wind swirled around them. "That sounds heavenly."

Just as he was about to lead her up the stairs, he jerked to a stop.

"Is everything okay?" Hope asked in surprise.

Enoch put a finger to his lips. His eyes were locked on the side of the mansion. Now that he thought about it, it was the side with the door that had been left open. He narrowed his gaze, positive he had seen movement a moment before. All the strange happenings from the past few months came slamming back into his brain.

"Enoch," Hope whispered. "You're scaring me."

Fumbling in his coat pocket, he grabbed his keys and put them in her palm. "Here. Unlock the door and go inside. I'll be right there."

"But—" Hope didn't get to finish her sentence because Enoch had already taken off.

He slid from shadow to shadow, determined to solve this mystery once and for all. However, when he got to the side door, no one was there. Enoch cursed under his breath and began to search the area.

"What's going on?" Hope asked, slightly out of breath.

Enoch jerked up. "I thought you were going inside?"

She gave him an incredulous look. "And let you deal with whatever was going on by yourself?"

Enoch shook his head. "For someone who doesn't like adventure, you didn't seem to pause at all."

"Maybe I just didn't like the idea of you being by yourself and getting hurt," she snapped. Turning on her heel, Hope began to march off. "I think maybe I'll call it a night."

Enoch lunged after her. "Hope," he said calmly, hoping the soft tone would draw her attention. He was grateful it worked. "I'm sorry," he said, turning her around. "I wasn't trying to offend you." He sighed and wrapped his arms around her waist. "I suppose I felt the same way as you did," he admitted. "I don't like the idea of you being in danger, which is why I wanted you in the apartment."

"But what if someone was here and snuck up behind you or something?" she asked, resting easily in his arms. It appeared her little snit was over, and Enoch relaxed.

"I wasn't even sure there was a person," he explained. "I thought I saw movement, but there's no one here and I don't see any evidence of anything, so I suppose it was my imagination."

Hope shivered against him. "All these things are starting to freak me out."

Enoch gave her a short but firm kiss. "Then let's quit worrying about it. I promised you a movie. Let's get to it."

She nodded and followed him inside. It wasn't long before they were curled up on his couch watching one of her favorite Christmas flicks. But despite how wonderful she felt tucked up against him and how much he hoped he could finagle another kiss or two out of her, Enoch couldn't get his mind off the image of someone sneaking around the house. He was almost positive he'd seen an intruder. *The question is...who?*

CHAPTER 10

The next day, Hope had just finished cleaning a guest suite when she found Emory pacing the floor of the hallway near the kitchen. "Hey, Em. What's going on?"

Emory stopped, her face solemn. "It happened again."

Hope frowned. "What do you mean?"

"One of my pies is missing." Emory threw up her arms. "Missing, Hope! How does an entire pie just go missing? First someone eats my nougat, and now this?" She shook her head and then brought her hands down to grip her hair. "It's driving me crazy! Something isn't right."

Before Hope could say anything, the doorbell rang and both girls jumped as if they'd been shocked with an electrical current.

Blowing out a long breath, Emory walked toward the kitchen. "Do you mind getting that? I'm not up to speaking to guests at the moment."

Hope watched her cousin stalk away, her mind spinning with all the thefts they'd had lately. *Why does someone keep sneaking food? And how does this all relate to the soap?* The doorbell rang again and Hope jumped into action. She couldn't stand around all day thinking about weird mysteries.

"Where's Bella?" Hope muttered as she walked as quickly as she could to the foyer. "This should fall under her domain."

Hope pulled the large door open and smiled widely. "Hello. Welcome to Cliffside Bed and Breakfast, also known as the Gingerbread Inn." She noticed the person didn't have any luggage with them, but continued with her speech anyway. "Are you here to check in?"

The young man's scowl was enough to curdle milk, and Hope had to stop herself from stepping backwards from the veracity of it. "I'm not here to check in. I'm here to serve you papers."

"Wait...what?" Hope didn't stop herself from backing up at this point. This was not what she expected at all.

"Can I help you?"

Hope let out a sigh of relief when Enoch's voice came from behind her. She turned to him and smiled gratefully. "I think there's been a misunderstanding," she whispered. "They said they have papers for us."

Enoch's eyebrows bunched up as he eyed the man on the doorstep. "What's this all about?"

"And just who are you?" the man asked, folding his arms over his chest.

"I'm Enoch Dunlap. I work here."

"Then this doesn't concern you," the man said. "I need to speak to a member of the family."

"I'm a member of the family," Hope said softly, stepping back up. Now that she wasn't alone, she wasn't quite as frightened as she was before, but she still didn't understand what was happening. "Please explain yourself."

"Which one are you?" the stranger demanded.

Hope felt herself bristle. What right did this man have to ask her questions like that? She folded her own arms in a defensive manner. "I don't feel safe giving you any information when you've been nothing but hostile. If you'll tell us your business, we'll do our best to get things taken care of."

He gave her a sardonic grin. "What? Don't you recognize me?"

Hope narrowed her gaze and frowned. "No. Should I?"

"George!" Grandma Claire cried from behind Hope. "What are you doing here?"

Hope turned to let her grandmother walk closer. Sheriff Davidson was with her, holding her elbow, and Hope would have smiled at the sight if she wasn't so worried about the current situation. "Who's George?" she asked.

"George Turnbridge," the man on the stoop said, tugging on the edge of his coat sleeves as if he were completely aloof from everything. "Hello, Claire. Long time, no see."

Grandma Claire rolled her eyes. "And it can be a lot longer, if necessary. Now what are you doing here?"

"I'm here on behalf of my family," he stated.

Who is George? Hope screamed in her mind. She had no idea what this all meant and no one seemed inclined to share.

"Okay..." Claire said, leaving an opening for him to continue.

Reaching into his coat pocket, he produced a thick envelope and held it out.

Sheriff Davidson was the first one to step forward to retrieve it. He scowled at the young man as he did so and Hope was grateful the look wasn't directed toward her. Stepping back inside, Sheriff Davidson handed the envelope to Grandma Claire, who quickly opened it and sighed.

"You're suing me? Really?"

"What?" Hope gasped.

Enoch's arm around her shoulders gave her an anchor that was more than welcome and she quickly stepped into his side, soaking up the strength he offered.

"On what grounds?" Bella called out from behind the crowd.

"Oh, good heavens," Hope mumbled. "This is turning into a circus."

Enoch snorted lightly, but otherwise stayed silent. Apparently he also wanted to figure things out.

"Haven't we had enough of this type of behavior?" Grandma Claire asked. "I didn't think it was legal to sue someone a second time."

"It's not," Bella said crisply, planting her hands on her hips. She eyed George like he was a bug of some kind. "I might not know the whole story here, but something smells fishy. What's this about?"

George had put a more pleasant look on his face as the crowd against him grew larger. "I'm here to represent my family, who want what is rightfully theirs. While we may have lost the first lawsuit, we have been watching you and feel it's time we interfered again." He nodded and tipped an imaginary hat. "I'll just let you work out the details yourself. I'll be in touch."

Hope quickly slammed the door behind him, then turned to her family and friends. "Okay...what in the world is going on? I feel like I'm in the twilight zone or something."

Bella snorted. "Sounds about right." She turned to Grandma Claire. "Spill it, Grams. Give up the goods."

Grandma Claire gave Bella a scolding look. "When you've won that Pulitzer, then you can talk to me like that."

Bella grinned. "Sorry. Got carried away. But seriously. What's going on?"

Grandma Claire sighed and gripping Sheriff Davidson's arm, turned around. "Let's take this to the kitchen. Emory will want to hear as well."

Hope watched them for a moment, not moving. Her heart was thudding painfully against her chest. *This December is turning out to be a nightmare!*

A warm hand grasped hers and squeezed twice.

Hope didn't try to stop the smile and turned to look at Enoch. "I'm more than a little freaked out," she admitted softly.

Enoch leaned in and kissed her temple. "Don't worry, we'll get it all fixed. Claire seems more annoyed than worried."

Hope nodded, knowing what he said was true. Standing up tall, she followed her family down the hall and into the bustling kitchen. It was time to solve a mystery.

"I DIDN'T REALIZE YOU would tell everyone!" Emory scolded as Hope and Enoch walked into the room last.

Hope's eyebrows shot up and she slapped her forehead. "Actually, I completely forgot!"

"Forgot what?" Bella quickly asked.

Enoch snorted a laugh. *That woman just can't help herself.*

Emory turned her glare to Bella, then sighed, her shoulders drooping. "A pie went missing this morning."

"Missing?" Sheriff Davidson jumped in. "How exactly does a pie go missing?"

"Easy, William," Claire said, patting his arm. "I'm sure she'll tell us all about it."

"As in, I made six pies and now there's only five," Emory snapped. "First the nougat, now the pie. Someone is either super hungry or is trying to sabotage me."

"How would eating your stuff sabotage you?" Bella asked, making a face.

Enoch felt like he was at a tennis match. His head just kept snapping from one person to the other, but until he had something to add, there was nothing else for him to do.

"Because it makes me look incompetent?" Emory asked. "Because they're trying to throw off my ability to perform in the gingerbread competition? Because they're trying to ruin my reputation?" She shook her head and held up her hands. "Take your pick."

Sheriff Davidson frowned. "So everything has been food-related?"

There was a pause as the group considered the question. Enoch wondered if he should share his suspicions, but Hope beat him to it.

"No."

All heads swiveled toward them.

"What do you mean?" Emory demanded. "And why haven't you said anything before now?"

Hope stepped back and Enoch twisted so she bumped into him. She was an adult, he trusted her to stand up to her cousin, but he also wanted her to know he was there. He knew her quiet personality made it difficult to speak up, but she could handle it.

"A jar of soap went missing a few days ago," she said softly. "And there was the morning the door was wide open."

"I'd forgotten about that," Emory murmured, her eyes glazing over as she considered everything.

"Now who's keeping secrets?" Bella shot out, shaking her head. She turned back to Hope. "What happened with the soap?"

Hope shrugged. "I don't know. But the closet is kept really organized, and one was missing when I went to grab supplies the other morning."

Bella tapped her lips. "So we have missing food, missing soap, open doors...anything else?"

"Moved tools," Enoch added. He shrugged sheepishly when everyone turned to him. "Nothing is missing, but I've had several times in the last few weeks when something was not where I left it."

Sheriff Davidson snorted. "Everything we're speaking of is circumstantial. Each and every one could have a plausible explanation."

"And I thought I saw a person the other night, but when I looked closer, no one was there," Enoch added.

Claire tsked her tongue and shook her head. "So we have nothing concrete."

"Maybe not, but we have another thing to add," Bella pointed out. She looked at Claire. "What's in the envelope?"

Claire sighed and worked her way to a seat at the dining table. "A bunch of poppycock," she said, tossing the envelope down.

"Maybe so, but you still owe us an explanation," Emory said, sliding in the next seat.

Sheriff Davidson stood next to Claire's chair, his arms folded over his barrel chest. It appeared he wasn't going anywhere.

Claire sighed again. "I suppose I do." She pinched her lips together. "A few years ago, my sister's children and grandchildren tried to sue me in order to take over the Gingerbread Inn."

Gasps of shock and outrage rang through the room and Enoch felt his eyebrows shoot up nearly to his hairline. He had no idea about any of this. It must have happened before his time.

"Did you know this?" Hope whispered.

Enoch shook his head. "Nope. I'm just as surprised as you."

"I thought you inherited the inn," Bella said brusquely.

Claire nodded. "I did, but only after my sister lost her rights to it."

"Maybe you better start from the beginning," Hope said, snuggling deeper into Enoch's side. It appeared she was settling in for the long haul.

He wasn't about to turn down the offer to hold her and wrapped both his arms around her. No matter what Claire was about to reveal, they would hear it together.

"You've always known the inn was passed from mother to daughter," Claire started. Her eyes went distant as she spoke. "My older sister should have rightfully inherited the inn." She shook her head. "But Peggy was a bit more...wild than I ever was. She didn't want anything to do with being tied down to this place. So when she turned eighteen, she left and never turned back."

"But how does that—" Bella started.

"Shhh!" Emory interrupted. "Let her finish."

Bella huffed, but quieted down.

Claire smiled and shook her head. "To shorten the story, when my father died, my mother started putting her own affairs in order, making sure everything was ready for when her own time came." Her face drooped and suddenly she looked much older. "It took us nearly a year to find Peggy, but when we did, she refused the inheritance."

Emory stood, breaking the silence, and went into the cooking area. When she came back, she was holding a hot cup of steaming liquid that she put in front of Claire.

Claire smiled gratefully. "Thank you, dear." She took a fortifying sip, then spoke again. "Peggy signed a legal affidavit saying she didn't want the inn and would never come after it in a court of law."

"I'm guessing that didn't apply to her posterity, however," Bella grumbled. She made a face when Emory smacked her arm.

"You're exactly right," Claire said. She set the mug down. "Peggy separated herself from the family so well that when she died years ago, I never even knew." Her bright blue eyes filled with tears and Sheriff Davidson cleared his throat. Claire glanced up before finishing. "So the point is, the family has found out the worth of this place and wants back in." She huffed. "They don't seem to want to be part of the family, just the money."

Hope shook her head. "But why? Why wouldn't they want to re-connect?"

Claire shook her head. "Your guess is as good as mine."

"I'm assuming they lost the first suit," Bella said, leaning her elbows onto the table. "And they can't sue you twice for the same thing." She tapped the wood. "So what are they suing for now?"

Claire searched the documents for a moment. "It would appear that they believe I am incompetent and senile," she said with disgust, dropping the papers. "They want to take over on the recommendation that I cannot handle this property myself."

Sheriff Davison murmured a few words under his breath that Enoch had to agree with.

"They have no stance, Claire," Enoch assured his employer. "Even if a court said you were in over your head, a judge would simply award it to your daughters."

Claire nodded. "Let's hope you're right, my boy. Because if I'm locked in the looney bin, having those *people* take over will make me crazy for real."

CHAPTER 11

"So what did you think of everything this afternoon?" Hope ventured as she and Enoch ate dinner in his apartment. She poked at her soup. "Talk about airing family laundry."

Enoch laughed. "That wasn't that bad. I told you my dad was a drunk and deadbeat." He tapped her foot with his and winked. "Looks like we're more alike than I thought."

Hope smiled. "I suppose so." She took a bite and chewed it thoughtfully. "But I still don't understand why they don't want to just reconcile. I mean...why come in like the enemy? Wouldn't they get further if they cleared the air?"

Enoch pursed his lips and shook his head. "I have no idea. Maybe Peggy had good reason for leaving her family?" He took a drink. "Do you know anything about Claire's parents? Were they good people?"

Hope shrugged. "As far as I know. I'm not much of an historian. I mean...Great Grandma inherited the inn from her mother, whom I think was the one to open it when she was widowed." Hope stirred her bowl. "All I know is it's passed down from mother to daughter. Peggy wanting out is kinda weird to me, but she must have had her reasons."

Enoch nodded. "I'm sure she did, but if no one's willing to share them, we'll never figure it out."

Hope sighed. "It's all such a mess. Why can't people just get along?"

He laughed. "If only life were so simple," he teased. Standing from the small table, he offered his hand. "Come on. I think chocolate and Christmas movies are in order tonight."

"You think that every night," Hope answered with a grin. She took his hand and stood. "Shouldn't we put the food away first?"

Enoch shook his head. "First off, I think that because I like dessert and I like holding you. Second, I think it's time you quit worrying about things and just enjoyed the holiday season for a bit."

Hope bit her lip as she followed him to the couch. "Well, so far this holiday season has been a little crazy. But I'll admit there's been a bright spot."

Enoch sat down, reaching forward to grab the remote, and smiled at her. "Oh, yeah? And what's that?" He tugged on her hand until she settled in next to him.

"Just this adorable guy who feeds me sugar and watches cheesy movies with me all the time." She sighed and settled her head on his shoulder. "He's made everything better."

She felt him press a kiss to the top of her head. "I feel the same way," he said against her hair.

The next twenty minutes were relatively quiet as they began an old movie, sinking further into the couch and each other's embrace. Enoch's fingers began to trail up and down Hope's arm, leaving goosebumps in its wake, and Hope felt her temperature begin to spike.

When she could stand his caresses no longer, she stirred and turned to face him, unsurprised when he was waiting for her. He immediately dropped his eyes to her lips, then back up, as if asking permission, which Hope was all too eager to give.

Just as he met her waiting mouth, a clattering from the garage below broke the intimate moment.

"What was that?" Hope asked breathlessly. She had straightened up and put a hand to her heart, where it was racing against her ribcage.

Enoch's face was hard as stone. "Stay here."

"We've been through this," she whispered fiercely as she followed him to the door. "I won't let you go alone."

Enoch blew out a harsh breath. "Fine, but please just...at least stay behind me?"

Hope nodded and together they crept down the stairs in the dark. At the bottom of the stairs, they paused. A rustling could be heard at the far end of the garage and Hope prayed she wouldn't pass out. It was possible they were about to solve all the mysterious happenings right now and she was terrified of what they might find.

Enoch leaned over and Hope saw the moonlight flash off something metal in his hand when he stood back up. Slowly, he stepped forward, not making any noise, then flipped on a light switch.

The sudden brightness had Hope shading her eyes, and by the time she opened them, it was too late.

"HEY!" Enoch shouted, rushing across the work space. He dove in and out of tables and furniture, heading for the far door, which was wide open.

"Enoch!" Hope cried out, running to follow him. By the time she got outside, Enoch was out of sight. Hope stalled, unsure which direction to go. She clasped her hands together and blew on them. The temperature had dropped significantly this evening and she wasn't wearing a coat. *Neither is Enoch*, she reminded herself. "Where are you?" she murmured, her fear boiling hard. Another couple of minutes went by without a sound. Just as Hope was about to go back to the main house for help, he walked back around the corner.

"Enoch!" Hope rushed over, wrapping her arms around him. "What happened? Did you find them?"

Enoch shook his head, his frustration evident in the hard lines of his face. "No. They got away."

Hope shivered.

"Come on, let's get you inside and warmed up." Enoch stepped back, took her hand and took her inside.

"You have to be freezing as well," Hope stammered through her chattering teeth.

Enoch shook his head. "Nah. I was running pretty hard."

They were quiet while they locked the doors and headed back up. Once inside, Enoch grabbed a blanket off the couch and wrapped it around her. "Want some cocoa?"

Hope shook her head. "No, thank you. I just want to know what's going on."

He sighed and nodded toward the seats. They both sat down and Hope turned on her hip to face him. Enoch ran a hand through his hair. "We must have made some noise at some point because just as I flipped on the light, they were darting out of the doorway."

"Could you tell who it was?" Hope asked.

"No. They were wearing a black sweatshirt with the hood up. The only thing I could tell was that they weren't very tall." Enoch scratched his chin.

"A woman, then?" Hope asked, surprised.

"Maybe." Enoch looked at her. "Why? Does that surprise you?"

She shrugged. "Not necessarily, I guess. It seems like stealing food and tools would be a guy thing."

"They haven't stolen any tools, though."

"You're right," Hope apologized. "I shouldn't be sexist. Sorry."

Enoch gave a light chuckle. "Forgiven." His face sobered. "But the question still remains. Who was it? And what are they after?"

ENOCH COULDN'T SEEM to get the intruder off his mind the rest of the evening, even with Hope snuggled up against him. He couldn't figure out how the person could disappear so quickly, and he hadn't managed to discover what they'd been doing in the shed either.

His mind was still churning the next day as he did a few odd jobs around the mansion during the morning hours. Hope had passed by him several times as she cleaned rooms and did her daily chores. Each time, she had smiled at him, helping to brighten his day, but he just couldn't seem to let go of the stranger.

The only upside he could find at the moment was the fact that they knew there was an actual intruder. Before, they had been unsure, but now Enoch had irrefutable evidence. He sighed and pushed a hand through his hair. *I guess I need to let Claire and the sheriff know.*

"GONE!" a woman screeched, breaking Enoch's thoughts. "IT IS GONE!"

"What in the world?" Bella came skidding around the corner to the bottom of the staircase, near where Enoch was working. She looked at him with wide eyes. "What's going on?"

Enoch shrugged and shook his head. "No idea."

A door slammed upstairs and hurried footsteps could be heard thundering down the hallway. Mrs. Harrison appeared at the top of the stairs, her face bright red. With a screech, she pointed her finger beyond Enoch and Bella. "YOU!"

Enoch turned to see Hope standing with a dusting cloth clutched to her chest. "Me?" she squeaked.

Enoch frowned, his protective instincts rearing to the surface. "What's this about, Mrs. Harrison?" he asked, pulling the attention to himself.

Instead of her usual elegant way of moving, Mrs. Harrison stomped down the stairs. "My ring," she ground out. "The ring my husband bought me on our twenty-fifth anniversary is missing." By this time she was standing at the bottom of the stairs next to Bella, who looked completely shell-shocked. Mrs. Harrison never took her eyes from Hope, glaring hard enough to intimidate the largest of football players, let alone quiet Hope. "You are the only one who has been in my room."

Hope's jaw dropped. "Are you suggesting *I* took your ring?"

The ashen look on Hope's face was too much and Enoch stepped in, right in Mrs. Harrison's line of sight. "Now, hold on," he said, putting his hands in the air. "Why don't you take a deep breath and we'll get this figured out."

"There is nothing to figure out," Mrs. Harrison argued. "She's the only one who's been in my room. She had to have taken it."

Bella stepped up next to Enoch, seeming to want to protect Hope from Mrs. Harrison's wrath as well. "Why would Hope steal your ring? Why would she want it?" Bella put her hands on her hips. "Don't you think blaming the housekeeper is a little too cliche?" She tsked her tongue, which only made Mrs. Harrison turn even more red.

Enoch's eyes grew wide. *She's gonna have a heart attack if she's not careful.*

Mrs. Harrison's eyes filled with tears and her hands clenched into fists. "Since she is the only one who has gone in my room, it's obvious she's only one it could be. That ring means more to me than you could ever know. I want it back, and I want it back now."

Enoch felt Hope's presence at his back and he held a hand back to hold her off. Right now he didn't want her anywhere near this madwoman.

"I didn't take your ring," Hope said, her voice soft and teary. "I promise I'm not a thief." She sniffed, then broke down into a quiet cry, and Enoch's heart just about broke.

He wanted so badly to turn around and take her in his arms, but until Mrs. Harrison had calmed down, he didn't dare take his eyes off of her. "When did you last see it?" he asked, hoping to turn the subject toward something helpful.

"I put it away last night when I went to bed," Mrs. Harrison said tightly. "I didn't wear it this morning before I went out. I came back from lunch with my son and it was gone." She let out a wail and slumped onto the stairs.

Enoch lunged forward to make sure she didn't hurt herself.

"I just want my ring!" Mrs. Harrison cried, burying her face in her arms.

"I'm going to call Antony," Bella announced, walking away from the crying woman and shaking her head.

Enoch nodded, then looked back down at Mrs. Harrison. *What now?* He looked across the foyer to Hope, whose beautiful skin was splotchy with red spots and wet with tears. She was shaking as she cried, and once again Enoch physically hurt for her.

"I didn't do it," Hope rasped. "I promise, I didn't do it."

Enoch nodded, still patting Mrs. Harrison's back. "I know, babe. I know."

"I didn't!" Hope cried out, her voice louder than before. "I would never take something that wasn't mine!"

Enoch nodded harder. "I know, Hope. No one thinks you did this."

Hope shook her head and backed away. "She—"

"Mother?" Antony's voice carried through the room and Mrs. Harrison wailed even louder, sitting up and throwing her arms toward her son.

"Antony! They have taken my ring! It is gone!"

Antony nodded to Enoch, then reached down and pulled his mother up into his arms. "It's going to be okay, Mom. Just take a deep breath and we'll get it all figured out."

"It's gone," she wailed. "Goooone!"

Antony nodded again. "I know, Mom. We'll figure it out. It's okay." He began leading her away from the foyer, toward the sitting room. "Let's sit down and we'll call the police and get it all taken care of." He glanced over his shoulder to Bella and raised his eyebrows.

"On it," she said quickly, rushing to the front desk phone.

"How the heck did he get here so fast?" Enoch muttered, scratching the back of his head.

"Are they going to arrest me?" Hope asked, her voice barely audible.

Crap. With the spectacle Mrs. Harrison was putting on with her son, Enoch had completely forgotten about Hope standing all by herself. He walked quickly toward her, his arms out. "No one is going to arrest you," he said soothingly.

She stepped away from him. "How do you know? How can I prove I didn't do it?" She folded in on herself. "I was in Mrs. Harrison's room this morning. I made her bed and cleaned her bathroom. My fingerprints will be everywhere!" Her breathing picked up and those blue eyes grew slightly wild.

Enoch kept his arms out. "Hope," he said firmly, catching her attention.

She turned to him, looking desperate.

"Sweetheart, no one is arresting you. Other than the crazy woman in the other room, no one thinks you took that ring." He took a step forward, treating her like he would a wild animal. "Come here," he said softly.

"Do you really believe me?" she asked, her voice calming down. She wiped her tears on her sleeve.

"I don't need you to say you didn't take it," Enoch said, closing the distance between them. He cupped her face and used his thumb to dry her cheeks. "I know you wouldn't do something like that," he assured her. "The Hope who is quickly stealing all my thoughts, time and attention would never do something like steal."

Hiccuping, she leaned into his chest and wrapped her arms around him. "Thank you," she said hoarsely against his shirt.

Rather than respond, Enoch just wrapped his arms around her and kissed the top of her head. *This is just one more thing to add to a long list of weird occurrences. I think it's time we took it more seriously. And I need to tell Sheriff Davidson about that prowler.*

CHAPTER 12

Hope's heart was racing so hard, she was afraid she might pass out at any moment. If it wasn't for Enoch's strength, she was sure she'd be a puddle on the floor. Her emotions were all over the place and she was struggling to keep herself in check. Right now, fear was winning over everything else, but there was a part of her that was completely offended that anyone would accuse her of stealing. *I've never done anything underhanded my entire life!* she cried inside. *Unless you count the one time I ate my brother's bacon when he wasn't looking. Otherwise, I've always been the boring one.*

She took in a shuddering breath. "What do you think is going on here?" she asked, still clutching Enoch. "It seems like nothing has gone right since I got here."

Enoch sighed and rubbed her back. "I don't know, but I think it's time we had another meeting." He pushed her back just enough to look at her face. "We need to tell everyone about the person we chased last night and this latest development."

Hope nodded. She forced herself to step away and pull herself together. "I'm sorry," she said, feeling like a complete fool. "I didn't mean to fall apart like that."

Enoch shook his head. "Don't you dare," he scolded. "No one would appreciate being attacked the way you were." A small grin pulled at his mouth. "Most would have fought back, and I have to admit that I'm glad I didn't have to pull apart a cat fight today."

Hope snorted and half-heartedly slapped his chest. "Like I'd ever be involved in a cat fight."

Enoch chuckled and wrapped his arms around her. "I know. And I'm grateful."

She sniffed. "I need to get a tissue and get myself together." Sighing, Hope stepped away from his comfort. "Give me a few minutes and we'll go join them in the sitting room."

Enoch nodded and stuffed his hands in his pockets.

Walking away from him was difficult when she still felt shaken, but Hope knew she must look like a mess, so she forced herself into the hallway bath. "Oh my gosh." She groaned when she looked at the mirror. "How can he stand to look at me?"

Shaking her head, she washed her face and blew her nose, praying the redness would go down quickly. "That's as good as it's going to get," she finally muttered, taking one last look in the mirror.

With a deep breath, she opened the door and headed back to Enoch. He looked so fantastic, waiting in the foyer for her. He was tall and thick, which was exactly why he was so comfortable to be held by. His dark hair looked almost blue in the bright lights of the foyer chandelier, and those dark blue eyes were fixated on her as she walked toward him. It was a heady feeling, knowing she was dating this amazing man. He was everything she could have dreamed of for herself. When her heart skipped a beat at his intense look, Hope began to realize something. *I've fallen,* she thought. *I've completely fallen in love with him. How in the world did it all happen so quickly?*

"Ready?" he asked, holding out his hand for her.

Hope gripped his palm, feeling as if she was admitting to much more than the moment. "I am," she answered. *As long as you're with me.* Together they walked to the sitting room, where Mrs. Harrison had finally settled down enough to speak without shrieking.

"You know," Enoch whispered in Hope's ear, "I still can't figure out how Antony got here so quickly. I don't know that Bella even had time to call him."

"He had to have already been here," Hope mused.

Enoch frowned. "But why?"

Hope shrugged until her attention was caught by Emory entering with a tray in her hands. Several steaming mugs and a plate of pastries sat in the middle. *Leave it to Emory to solve this with food.* She gasped quietly. "Could Antony have been here with Em?"

Enoch's eyebrows went up. "Well, well, well..." he murmured, then chuckled. "Could the barriers be coming down between the enemies?"

Hope made a face. "Huh. It would make sense...sort of. I mean, their tension is insane, so..."

Enoch nodded thoughtfully. "Yeah. I've wondered from the beginning if their hate wasn't quite as strong as they claimed."

Hope pinched her lips between her teeth. "I shouldn't laugh, considering the situation, but I find that kind of funny."

Enoch smiled and gave her a squeeze. "It would certainly be entertaining."

"Claire?"

The entire room turned to the voice as Sheriff Davidson stormed into the room. His scowl was fierce and Hope had to bite her tongue to keep from shouting that she was innocent. "What's this about another thief?"

"Another?" cried Mrs. Harrison. Her face crumpled. "What type of place have you put me in, Antony? A place where they steal things willy-nilly? Have you no more care for me than that?"

"Mother, stop," Antony said firmly. "You knew about the missing candy. You were there when Emory accused me."

Mrs. Harrison sniffed. "As if you would do such a thing."

"I could say the same thing about Hope," Bella shot out.

"Hear, hear!" Grandma Claire responded.

Bella gave Mrs. Harrison a defiant look. "I'm not worried about being in your good graces, nor am I too soft-spoken to fight back," she stated when Mrs. Harrison glared. "You came downstairs and threw out accusations like they were nothing when you have no real evidence."

"I do have evidence!" Mrs. Harrison argued.

Hope stiffened, then relaxed when Enoch rubbed her shoulders.

"Then I, for one, would like to hear it," Sheriff Davidson said. He walked over to a chair and plopped down before removing his hat. "Excuse me, Claire," he said sheepishly. "I should have taken it off at the door."

Grandma Claire nodded. "Nothing to worry about, William. I just want this solved."

Hope's vision began to swim again, but she forced a small smile when Grandma looked her way and gave her an encouraging nod. *Looks like my family is on my side,* she thought gratefully.

"Start at the beginning, please," the sheriff huffed, opening a small notebook and preparing to take notes.

Mrs. Harrison sat up, ramrod straight, put her nose in the air and explained everything again. "So you see, Sheriff," she said in her slightly accented voice. "It could only have been the housekeeper."

The sheriff grunted, then looked to Hope. "Ms. Hope. Did you ever see this ring?"

Hope shrugged. "Not that I know of. I made her bed and cleaned the bathroom. None of that involved her jewelry."

He nodded and looked around the room. "Is it possible another guest could have done it?" he asked, then put up his hand when everyone began to argue at once. "Now, hold on. Nothing's going to get fixed if we all fight each other."

"SHERIFF!" ENOCH CALLED out, knowing he needed to speak up. When Sheriff Davidson looked his way, Enoch stepped forward a little. "Last night Hope and I saw a prowler on the property."

Someone gasped, but Enoch kept his eyes on the sheriff. "We were watching a movie when I heard noise in the workshop."

"Why didn't you say something earlier, son?" the sheriff asked, sitting up taller with a frown.

Enoch rubbed the back of his neck. "Truth was, I wasn't quite sure what to do about it. But while I was fixing that outlet in the front entryway, I decided I should tell Claire, only to have Mrs. Harrison come down the stairs, upset about her ring."

Sheriff Davidson nodded. "Did you see who it was?" he asked. "What were they doing?"

Enoch shook his head. "I don't know who it was. They were wearing a black hoodie that covered their face and upper body. But they were several inches shorter than I am and judging from the way their clothes hung on them, they're thin."

Mrs. Harrison sniffed delicately and used a handkerchief to wipe her nose. "Why would they take my ring?"

"Did you see them take anything?" Sheriff Davidson asked.

Enoch shook his head again. "Not that I can tell. They were messing with something on one of the workbenches when I found them. I chased them out the door, but they disappeared before I could get close enough to see who it was."

The sheriff ignored Mrs. Harrison's grumbling and scratched his slightly scruffy chin. "This is getting more and more complicated," he muttered. Shaking his head, he slapped his thighs and stood. "I think maybe I need to call in a favor."

"What, William? What are you going to do?" Claire asked, a tone of worry in her voice.

"I've got a friend in the county over who's a detective," Sheriff Davidson said with a sigh. "I think maybe we could use his expertise about now."

"Oooh," Bella said with an excited grin. "Can I play detective too?"

"Bella, this is serious," Emory jumped in. "Someone is stealing things and sneaking into the mansion."

Bella rolled her eyes. "I get that. I'm not an idiot."

"Well, you're sure acting like one," Emory snapped.

"Hey!" Bella cried.

"Ladies," Claire interrupted, clapping her hands for attention. "Now is not the time for your squabbles."

"Now is the time to find my ring," Mrs. Harrison inserted. "When can your detective arrive?" she asked Sheriff Davidson. "I will only be here for another couple of days."

"Thank heavens," Hope muttered under her breath, making Enoch hold back laughter.

He tugged her closer, tucking her under his chin.

"I'm sure everything will work out in time for your departure," Antony said, patting his mother's hand.

"Oooh," she moaned. "If only I had not come on this trip. I would still have my ring and my sanity."

There was no missing Bella's eye roll at the woman's dramatics. Even Antony had to cough in order to cover his laughter.

"I guess I'll be on my way, then," Sheriff Davidson said, working his way to the front door.

"Here, Sheriff," Emory said, stalling his progress. She wrapped a croissant in a napkin. "Something for the road."

The sheriff smiled and tipped his head. "Thank you, Ms. Emory. I sure do love your cooking."

She smiled back and Enoch noticed Antony scowl slightly. "You're welcome. And I love anyone who loves my baking, so I guess it all works out."

The sheriff chuckled, tipped his hat to the rest of the room and left.

"Mrs. Harrison," Claire said, breaking the silence.

The woman raised her eyebrows in response.

"It would appear that you have had a difficult time since you arrived at my inn and that just won't do." Claire climbed to her feet. "What do you say to you and I taking a stroll along the boardwalk and me showing you the best place to eat in Seagull Cove?" She smiled sweetly. "All on me, of course."

Mrs. Harrison patted her hair, looking pleased with the offer, but holding back slightly. "I do not know, Mrs. Simmons. It has been difficult—"

"Grandma," Hope jumped in. "I don't think you should be walking that far, should you?" She looked to Enoch, who was also slightly concerned. The boardwalk was close to the mansion, but it wasn't smooth footing the whole way. Years of water and wind had warped some of the boards, and for someone like Claire, they could be treacherous.

"Poppycock," Claire declared. "I've got my cane. I'll be fine." She looked back to Mrs. Harrison. "What do you say, Lucia? Should we leave the young'uns to figure out the mystery?"

Mrs. Harrison hesitated, then jumped to her feet. "I believe that is a good idea." Not bothering to look at the rest of the group, she linked arms with Claire and the two of them headed toward the coat closet.

Everyone else watched them go, no one speaking.

"I didn't see that coming," Bella finally said when the front door was closed.

Emory shook her head. "I wouldn't have believed it if I didn't see it with my own eyes."

"She's not so bad once you get to know her," Antony said, shoving his hands in his back pockets.

Emory's cheeks turned pink and she fiddled with her apron strings. "I'm sure you're right."

"That ring was my father's last gift to her before he passed," Antony continued.

Emory's eyebrows drooped at the sides. "I'm so sorry. No wonder she's devastated."

Antony nodded slowly. "Thank you." He looked around, seeming to suddenly realize they had an audience. Clearing his throat, he jabbed his thumb toward the front entrance. "I guess I better be going, then, huh?"

Emory's cheeks were even brighter now and Enoch pinched his lips together. "Uh, yeah. Thanks for coming to...help," she stammered, her body language growing more awkward with every word she spoke.

Antony nodded again. He was beginning to look like a bobblehead doll, as he slowly worked his way to the doorway. His eyes darted around the room and his usual cockiness was clearly gone at what he saw. "I'm sorry for her outburst, especially to you, Hope. I'm sure we'll get it all figured out." Without waiting for an answer, Antony spun on his heel and darted out of the room. The front door opened and closed only moments later.

Slowly, as if it were planned, every head turned to look at Emory.

Her blue eyes widened and she backed up a couple of steps. "What?" she finally demanded, her voice slightly squeaky.

When no one spoke, Emory hurried to the tray, picked up all the dishes and rushed back to the kitchen.

Enoch looked to Hope, who was holding her hands over her mouth, amusement clear in her eyes. He was glad to see the fear of only moments before gone.

"Well..." Bella huffed, letting herself fall back into the couch cushions. "I think we might have more than one mystery to solve." She turned to look at Enoch and Hope. "For instance, why was Antony in the kitchen with Emory when I went in to get his number?" She raised an eyebrow. "And what were they doing that made them so flustered they couldn't speak like competent adults when I first ran in there?"

"I have no doubt you'll figure it out soon enough," Hope said with a smile.

Bella tapped her nose. "It *is* my job after all."

CHAPTER 13

"Hope?"

Hope stopped polishing the bannister and looked down the stairs to see Emory standing at the bottom. "Hmm?"

"Have you seen Bella?"

Hope frowned and wracked her brain. "Isn't she at the front desk?"

Emory huffed. "No. But she should be."

"She didn't tell anyone where she was going?" Hope asked, worry slithering down her spine. It had been a couple of days since the ring theft, but there had continued to be problems around the mansion. Her cleaning cart had been moved into a bad position while Hope was inside a room once, blocking some guests. Grandma had almost tripped over a garden rake on the side of the house, but the shed with the supplies had been found locked up tight. And food continued to disappear from the kitchen. Now that Emory was paying close attention, she found everything from apples and bananas to a bag of chocolate chips slipping from her shelves.

Someone is going to get hurt if we don't get things settled soon, Hope thought, which was exactly why Bella's disappearance had Hope worried.

"No." Emory tapped her foot impatiently. "That detective is supposed to be here this afternoon and if Bella misses him, she's gonna give us what-for."

Hope chewed on the inside of her cheek. "Have you called her cell?"

Emory gave her cousin a wry look.

"Right. Sorry." Hope shook her head. "Of course that would be the first thing you would do." She tapped her lip. "I can't think of how else to get a hold of her." Hope pinched her lips together. "You don't think our criminal did something to her, do you?"

Emory snorted. "Stealing food hardly makes someone a kidnapper, Hope."

"They took jewelry as well," Hope pointed out.

Emory nodded. "True, but it's still not the same."

"Okay." Hope shrugged. "Maybe find Grandma? Maybe they're working on something together?"

Emory nodded. "I didn't think of that. Good call." She began to walk away. "He's coming at two. Do you plan to be there?"

Hope made a face. "I probably don't have a choice. They'll need to hear my side of things."

Emory's look turned sympathetic. "I'm sorry about Mrs. Harrison. She can be...difficult, but she really is a nice woman at heart."

Hope studied her cousin. The all-work, no-play woman had taken a step back for the moment and it was refreshing to see some compassion. *Just how much time has she been spending with Mrs. Harrison, and more importantly...her son?* "I'll keep that in mind, thank you."

Emory cleared her throat. "Good. I'll go look for Grandma."

Hope glanced at the large grandfather clock in the foyer to check the time. "Half-hour," she muttered to herself, going back to wiping down the bannister. "Half-hour and we'll hopefully get all these problems on the right track."

Despite being busy with work, the time went slowly for Hope. Her worries that an outsider would believe Mrs. Harrison's claim that Hope was the thief had resurfaced and were percolating inside her stomach as the clock eventually chimed the hour.

"Has Detective Gordon shown up yet?" Enoch asked as he walked into the inn.

Hope couldn't help but smile. She hadn't seen him since breakfast, and his presence always brought her comfort. "No, but I'm sure he'll be here soon," she said, walking his way.

Enoch grinned and gave her a quick kiss. "Hey," he said softly.

"Hey, yourself, stranger," she teased.

His smile widened. "I've spent the morning pouring over the garden shed, trying to figure out how the person got inside." He scratched the back of his head.

"And?"

Enoch shook his head. "They didn't. At least as far as I can tell." He snorted. "I guess it's possible the rake isn't even ours. I don't really work on the grounds, so I don't know how many we have, but nothing appears to be missing inside and the place was closed up tight. But why would someone bring a rake from somewhere else and then leave it here?"

"Why seems to be the question of the day," Hope agreed. "Why would someone steal food, but leave tools behind? And what about the cleaning supplies? That doesn't fit with the other two either." She rubbed her temples, a headache forming. "It just doesn't seem to make sense. The two don't go together."

"I agree," Enoch stated. "It almost seems like we have someone with multiple personalities running around." He tilted his head. "Or just several different people. But that seems crazier yet."

Hope opened her mouth to answer, but the doorbell rang, cutting her off. "That must be him," she murmured, stepping away from Enoch to answer the door.

"Is this the Cliffside Bed and Breakfast?" a tall, handsome man, who appeared to be in his thirties, asked from the front step. His light brown hair blew across his dark eyes, creating a striking contrast, and his square jawline paired nicely with his equally square shoulders.

"It is," Hope answered. "Are you Detective Gordon?"

He nodded. "Guilty as charged," he admitted with a grin. "I'm assuming you're one of the granddaughters." He chuckled. "You don't look like Bill's description of Mrs. Simmons."

Hope laughed lightly, relaxing at his easy-going demeanor. "You guessed it." She opened the door wider. "Come on in." She noticed just how tall he was as he walked past her. "And thank you for saying I don't look as old as my grandmother. I think my ego would have been shattered."

Detective Gordon laughed, a deep rumbling tone that seemed to fill the foyer. "I imagine it would for anyone." He looked around and whistled low. "Nice place ya got here."

Hope shrugged and slipped her hand into Enoch's as he came up behind her. "Thank you. It's been in the family a long time and we like it."

"I'll bet." Detective Gordon eyed Enoch. "You must be the boyfriend. Enoch, was it?"

Enoch stepped forward and shook Detective Gordon's hand. "You've obviously done your homework."

Hope's cheeks were flaming. Although she had referred to her and Enoch as together, she'd never actually used the word boyfriend. *I don't know why that bothers me. I'm falling in love with the man, for heaven's sake. Calling him my boyfriend shouldn't be a big deal.*

But it did feel big, especially since she and Enoch had never truly defined their relationship. His casual agreement with Detective Gordon, however, let her know that he didn't mind the title.

And if he doesn't mind, why should I?

"I'M PRETTY SURE EVERYONE'S going to be waiting in the ballroom," Hope said, waving an arm in that direction. "Why don't you follow us?"

Detective Gordon nodded and Enoch took Hope's hand, leading the way. Just like she said, the room was full of a waiting audience.

"Detective, this is my cousin Emory."

He nodded. "Miss."

Emory smiled. "Welcome. Can I get you a donut? I made some fresh this morning."

Enoch chuckled at Detective Gordon's surprised look. "I suppose I'm talking to the baker, then."

Emory's smile widened. "Correct."

"In that case, I'd be a fool to turn down anything you made. Bill says you're cooking comes straight from heaven."

Emory's cheeks pinked up and the man at her side stepped forward. Enoch bit back laughter when Antony put a proprietary hand on her back.

"Antony Harrison," he said, leaning forward to shake hands. "Also a baker."

Detective Gordon responded in kind. "Nice to meet you. It's your mom who's missing the ring, correct?"

Antony nodded toward the woman in question. "This is my mother, Lucia Harrison."

"Ma'am," the detective said. "Don't worry. We'll find your things."

Mrs. Harrison sniffed. "I hope so."

"This is my grandmother, Claire Simmons," Hope continued. She looked around while the two shook hands. "Where's Bella?"

"Coming!" Bella bounded into the room, her strawberry blonde hair blowing behind her. "Whew! I made it." She skidded to a stop, her mouth gaping as she looked at Detective Gordon. Her open mouth snapped into a wide smile. "Well, hello..."

This time Enoch lost the battle and he tried to cover his snorting laughter with a cough, especially when Hope elbowed him in the ribs. He knew he wasn't fooling anyone, though. When Antony began to sound like he was choking, Enoch felt a little better.

"You must be Isabella," Detective Gordon said smoothly, his eyes focused on her.

"I must be, indeed," she said, sashaying into the room. "And you are?"

"Detective Gordon." He smiled. "Henry Gordon. But everyone calls me Hank."

"Nice to meet you, Hank."

"How come he didn't ask us to call him Hank?" Enoch whispered for Hope's ears alone.

"Stop it," she hissed, though her shoulders were shaking with amusement.

Mrs. Harrison sighed loudly. "Where is the Sheriff? Is he not coming?"

Hank pulled himself away from Bella and turned to face the woman. "He should be here shortly," Hank explained. "He had a call in town he needed to finish."

While his back was turned, Bella turned to Hope and held up her left hand, pointing to the ring finger. "He's not wearing a ring!" she mouthed to Hope.

Hope smiled and nodded. "Go for it!" she mouthed back.

Enoch had to turn away. He was about to lose control and he didn't want Hope to get angry at him. *Good luck to Hank,* Enoch thought. *He might need it.*

"Why don't we go around and you can all tell me your side of things, hm?" Detective Gordon suggested. "Bill has heard all this before, so when he gets here we can jump into the thick of it."

The next hour was spent taking turns doing one-on-ones with the detective. Somewhere in the middle, Sheriff Davidson showed up and promptly sat next to Claire, where Emory plied him with more baked sweets.

Enoch sat in a chair with Hope beside him. His knee bounced restlessly in his desire to be out of there.

Hope put her hand on his thigh. "What's wrong?" she whispered.

"Just bored," Enoch stated. "Sorry." He forced his limb into submission.

"You don't find the mystery thing fascinating?" she teased.

Enoch snorted. "If we were actually solving a mystery, that would be fine. Instead, we're sitting here doing nothing."

Hope laughed quietly. "Have you always been a mover and a shaker?"

He grinned sheepishly and rubbed the back of his neck. "Probably. I don't have to move fast, but I don't like to sit still." He tilted his head to the side. "I guess that's what's nice about woodworking. There's always something to do."

She patted his leg. "I don't mind sitting still once in awhile. One of these days, when I have a job, I'll buy that rocking chair in the corner of your workshop. Then I'll sit in it every night and read my stories with a cup of tea."

Enoch looked at her. He knew exactly which rocking chair she was referring to. It was a simple design with a few small leaves in the corners for decoration. It was one of the first things he'd made when he got back to Seagull Cove, and for some reason, he hadn't been able to bring himself to sell it.

While it wasn't necessarily any different than his other work, in fact, if anything, it was more plain than his other work. But making it had helped fix what was broken inside of him when he'd arrived in Seagull Cove with no money and no home. The rest of him wasn't worth much, but his hands had created something beautiful. Simple, but beautiful, and it felt precious to him. It felt like a piece of himself had been repaired and so he'd never put it on the website or taken it to any farmer's markets. Instead, it had sat in the corner, waiting for him to decide its fate.

The image of Hope rocking away with a book in her hands, a blanket on her lap struck him like lightning. Someone like Hope wouldn't just rock while she read. She would also rock her babies, maybe even singing as she moved back and forth, her eyes closed and a sweet, serene smile playing on her plush mouth.

His desire to be a part of that picture was overwhelming. His soul seemed to crave the domesticity it suggested. The peace, the joy and the happiness having Hope permanently in his life would entail. He wanted it. He wanted it more than he could express.

But it's too soon! his mind screamed. *You've only been with her a few weeks. People don't fall in love and decide their future in a matter of days...do they?*

"You just say the word," he finally rasped, "and that rocker is yours."

Hope's face lit up before she bumped his shoulder. "I can't just take something like that from you. I'll find a way to pay you."

I'll take you up on that, he thought. *Hopefully it won't cost more than you're willing to give.*

CHAPTER 14

Now that the detective was helping out with the case, Hope found herself feeling much better about the situation, though odd circumstances still occurred around the mansion. Especially around Hope.

Even though Detective Gordon hadn't made a move to accuse her of anything, Hope's concern was still high. Her cart was often in a mess in the morning, when she went to pick it up, even though she'd organized it the night before.

Her towels were sometimes found on the floor in a messy pile, requiring Hope to rewash them. One time she even found a garbage bag torn open with the contents spread across the hallway.

Thank goodness no one was around at that time of day, she thought bitterly. "Why is everything happening to me?" she muttered. "It doesn't make any sense." *And if something else goes missing, I doubt I'll be able to convince anyone of my innocence.*

The ring was still gone and each day that passed only made Hope more tense. The gingerbread competition was in a few days on Christmas Eve and the inn would be filled with people for weeks, coming to see the displays and enjoy a treat. Which would only make it harder to catch the culprit for all the troubles.

The door to the room she was cleaning squeaked open and Hope gasped, spinning to see who was coming in.

"Enoch!" She blew out a breath. "How many times are you going to sneak up on me?" she scolded.

He chuckled and looked around the room. "As many as I can, I suppose. I don't know how you don't hear me coming."

She gave him a playful scowl. "I'm not listening for sneaky handymen to come scare me to death."

"Maybe you should."

Hope rolled her eyes. "So noted," she said dryly, then paused. "Did you need something?"

His grin was quick and anticipation filled Hope's chest. "I always need something from you," he quipped.

Hope laughed quietly. "I'm working."

Enoch nodded and walked in the rest of the way, but not before checking the hallway behind him. "Me too," he said, hurrying across the room to gather her in his arms. "But one little kiss isn't going to hurt anything, is it?"

Hope gave a beleaguered sigh. "I suppose not." She wrapped her arms around his neck. "But only one."

Enoch gave her a firm, lingering kiss. "Your kisses are kind of like potato chips," he whispered after pulling back.

"What?" Hope frowned, completely unsure of where he was going with this, but the smirky grin on his face said he was teasing her.

"You know...betcha can't eat just one?" He kissed her again. "One is never enough with you," he murmured against her lips.

"That was a terrible joke," she said breathlessly.

"Yeah, but it got me another kiss, didn't it?"

Hope laughed. "I suppose it did."

Enoch glanced toward the bathroom. "I was told I needed to come fix a—" He stiffened and his face turned away from her.

"Crud," Hope muttered. "We've been caught, haven't we?"

Enoch shook his head, then put a finger to his lips. Letting go of her, he walked to the wall and slowly put his ear against it.

"Enoch. What are you—"

Again, he cut her off with a finger to his lips.

Sighing, Hope finally walked over and copied his actions. Within seconds, she gasped. Shuffling could be heard behind the wall and if she wasn't mistaken, someone was muttering to themselves. "Please tell me that's a really large mouse," she said in a barely audible voice.

Enoch shook his head solemnly. After listening for another moment, he took her hand and guided Hope out of the room. She didn't pay any attention to the fact that her job wasn't done or that Enoch needed to fix something. All she could think about was the fact that a person was in the walls of the mansion.

"I can't believe I didn't think of it before," Enoch muttered angrily as he hurried down the stairs.

"What?" Hope panted as she worked to keep up with him.

"The secret passages."

"What?"

Enoch stopped and Hope skidded along beside him. "There are passages in the house," he stated.

"How come I've never heard of them?" Hope demanded. "My family owns this place and I've never heard Grandma say anything about secret passages."

Enoch shrugged and shook his head before taking off again. "I don't know. Maybe she didn't want you to get hurt, or maybe she didn't think of it, but they're there. I've been in them. In fact, I think most of the kids in town have been in them at one time or another." He tugged her into the laundry room. "I can remember an outside entrance that we used to dare each other to go in as kids. You know, like it was some kind bravery symbol or something."

"This is unbelievable," Hope muttered. "The whole town knew, but the family didn't?"

"I can't help you there," Enoch murmured distractedly. He let go of her hand and felt around on the wall just beside the washer. "I'm pretty darn sure there's an entrance...got it!"

Hope's eyes widened and her jaw nearly hit the floor. "Oh my goodness..." she breathed.

A tiny door, almost too small for them to pass through, had popped open in the room. A cold breeze came from the passage and there were no lights inside, making the hallway dark and foreboding.

Enoch turned on the flashlight on his cell phone and stepped forward.

"Wait!" Hope cried, grabbing his arm. "You're not going in there, are you?'

Enoch looked at her like she was crazy. "Of course I am. How else are we going to catch them?"

"Isn't that why the detective's here? Shouldn't we call him?"

"They'll be gone by the time he gets here," Enoch huffed. Closing his eyes, he sighed. "Look, Hope. I want this solved once and for all, and I know you do too." He stepped back toward her and kissed her forehead. "Stay here, and if I'm not out in a few minutes, call for help. Okay?"

"You can't really expect me to just let you go inside!" she squeaked.

He gave her a patient look. "Yeah, I can, and I do." He stepped away. "Now hang tight. I'll be back before you know it."

Before Hope could respond again, Enoch disappeared into the dark. She stood frozen to the spot, completely shocked at everything that had just happened. But as her mind slowly caught up with the situation, her heart began to painfully thud in her chest. "There's no way I'm letting the man I love walk straight into the hands of a criminal," she said through gritted teeth. Turning on her cell flashlight, she gripped the device with white-knuckled fingers and walked to the entrance. "For once in your life," she scolded herself, "be brave."

ENOCH STEPPED AS CAUTIOUSLY as he could, not knowing quite how well the sound would carry now that he was inside the walls of the house. It had been at least fifteen years since he'd crawled around in here, and doing it as a scared teenage boy meant he didn't pay a lot of attention to where he was.

Wracking his brain, he wiped a cobweb off his face, desperately trying to gain his bearings so he could head toward the upstairs bedroom the suspect had been in. A few minutes in, he found a row of stairs and carefully made his way to the top. He could hear the wood creaking and it made him want to groan at how loud it was, but he bit his tongue instead. *Hopefully they'll just think it's the sounds of an old house.*

Something skittered across the path in front of him and Enoch's already racing heart nearly popped through his ribcage. He paused a moment to catch his breath. *Keep it together, Dunlap.*

Once he felt in control of himself, he moved forward again. "It's got to be around here," he murmured to himself, feeling the walls for any possible doorways. His cell light helped, but didn't shine far enough to light more than a few feet in front of him.

He swept his hands across the wall, searching meticulously for any nook or cranny, so he could figure out exactly where he was. The map in his mind said he should be close to the room he started in, but there was nothing around him to indicate he was correct.

With a small sigh, he kept working his way down the long passage. Finally, his fingers felt a strange bump in the wall. Eagerly, he shined his light on it and realized he'd found a peephole. Carefully he pulled it back, holding his breath the whole time, and peered through. A dark, empty room met his gaze. From the looks of the pristine bed, it was one Hope had already cleaned for the day.

Enoch put the stopper back in the hole. "Onto the next one, then."

He walked on, until he found the next peephole. Again he looked inside, this time finding the room he and Hope had shared a sweet kiss in before hearing the noise in the walls. "Bingo." Enoch stepped back, replugging the hole, and looked around. "But now what?" He looked at the floor, seeing footsteps in the dust, but there were so many, there was no way to pick out anything useful.

Straightening, he looked both ways down the dark hallway, straining his ears. Nothing came to him but thick silence and heavy darkness. Huffing, Enoch put his hand on his hip. "There's got to be something around here. And where the heck did the thief go?"

Noting that the passage he had come through was too small for him to have passed someone and not known it, Enoch looked forward with a nod. "Just gotta keep moving," he grumbled quietly.

Determined to succeed in this search, he pushed forward. A few more peepholes along the way showed him there was a way to see into every room on the second story of the home. He shook his head. *I don't even want to know what illicit information has been overheard over the years.*

After what seemed like an eternity, he came to another set of stairs. Enoch cautiously put his foot on the bottom step, but it groaned loudly and he pulled back. He listened hard to hear if anyone would do something about the noise, but was met with the same intense silence he had had from the beginning.

"Unless I missed something, the perpetrator has to be up here," he told himself. Grabbing a hammer from the tool belt hanging at his hips, he moved his foot to the opposite corner of the step and began the upward climb.

The wooden steps made far too much noise for his liking, but if the thief really was upstairs, there was no way for them to get away except to pass by Enoch, so he quit worrying about it and just walked.

A door stood at the top. Refusing to put down the hammer, Enoch slipped his phone into his pocket, losing the light, but keeping his weapon. Reaching out, he felt for the door handle and slowly turned it. The door squeaked softly and swung open as if the hinge had been recently oiled.

When nothing jumped out at him, Enoch grabbed for his phone, shining the light around. The roof was pitched sharply, letting Enoch know he had reached some kind of attic. There was an attic inside the mansion, but this was not the space he usually entered when going up there.

Instead of all the storage they kept in the attic, he found a small wooden table and two chairs. There was a window in the far wall, but it was so covered in grime and dust that it barely let in any light.

Looking closer, Enoch realized there were dishes on top of the table and he stepped toward it to investigate when something hit him in the face. He swatted away what he thought was a cobweb, but the object was heavier...like a string.

Inspiration struck and he grabbed the string and tugged, flooding the space with light. "What in the world?" The first thing he noticed was a pile of musty, old blankets in the corner, along with a ratty pair of boots.

The dishes he had noticed previously were chipped and broken, all except for a beautifully painted pie dish. Smears of fruit were left in the bottom, but otherwise it had been licked clean.

Enoch shook his head. "Guess we know where the pie went," he muttered, looking around some more. It was apparent someone had been living in the space. "Where are they?" he asked himself.

Nothing else he saw revealed anything about the person who had been camping in the mansion's hidden attic, so Enoch turned to go back. Tucking the pie plate under his arm, he made his way down the staircase and into the hallway he had been in before.

He squished his lips to the side, trying to figure out the best move, when a crash and scream had him running in reckless abandon. *That was Hope!* he yelled internally, recognizing her voice.

He couldn't seem to move fast enough toward where the sound had come from, as he ran along the deserted hallway. More crashing came from in front of him and it took a moment to realize it was on the other side of the wall.

Skidding to a stop, he quickly set down the pie plate and stuffed the hammer back in his belt.

"What is wrong with you?" Hope screamed, just as another crash sounded.

"HOPE!" Enoch bellowed, pouding on the wall between them. His hands ran over the entire surface in front of him, growing more and more frantic as he heard a wrestling match going on in the bedroom on the other side. "HANG ON, HOPE! I'M COMING!" he shouted.

With every second that ticked by, his heart fell a little further. The only way the other person could have gotten to Hope was if there was some kind of door, so he knew it had to be there. *But please let me find it in time.*

CHAPTER 15

Hope had no idea where she'd taken a wrong turn, but despite walking for several minutes, she hadn't seen or heard anything from Enoch. Her knees were shaking so hard she was sure she would end up collapsing to the floor and just waiting for him to come rescue her. She scoffed at herself. "Such an idiot. You completely fell apart when Mrs. Harrison said you stole the ring. And now you can't even walk through a dark, spooky secret passage." She snorted at herself.

A shuffling sound in front of her made the smile drop, however, and her fears rose again to the surface. Hope slowed down and tucked her flashlight into her pocket. Easing along the wall, she heard noises and paused to listen.

Someone was on the other side of the wall. *But are they a guest or the person we're tracking?* There was no way for her to know and without any light, she couldn't see how to get into the room either. Skimming her fingers along the wall, Hope searched for something to help her. Surely there had to be ways into the rooms. Otherwise the culprit wouldn't have been able to move around so easily.

When nothing could be found, Hope sighed heavily. Turning her back to the wall, she slid down, putting her head in her hands. "This is all so hopeless," she moaned, banging her head against the wall, unconcerned with whether or not the other person heard her. Without warning, she felt the wall give way behind her and Hope fell onto her back with a bang and a loud gasp.

Her head spun for a moment from hitting the ground, but she climbed to her feet, shaking off the dizziness.

"Unbelievable," came a growling female voice from across the room.

Hope zeroed in on the words to see Trisha standing next to the dresser of the guest bedroom. The guest's private knicknacks were strewn all over the top of the dresser, and Hope realized Trisha was about to steal something else.

"What are you doing?" she cried, stepping forward. "AHH!" Hope screamed and ducked as Trisha threw a small garbage can at her.

"Why are you still here?" Trisha screamed, scrambling for something else to throw.

"STOP! Trisha stop!" Hope called out, ducking beside the bed. "I don't understand what's going on!"

"Of course you don't," Trisha said, her voice dark and low. "You're an imbecile! You shouldn't even be here! If that stupid sheriff would do his job, you'd be in jail and Enoch would be free to pay attention to me again!"

A light bulb went on in Hope's head and she felt like the imbecile Trisha said she was, for not recognizing the problem. "You're in love with him, aren't you?" She winced as something else smashed against the wall, breaking into a thousand shards. *She's gonna trash all of Grandma's antiques if I don't stop her.* Another decoration exploded against the wall, and this time dirt and leaves scattered. "Oh my gosh, this is ridiculous."

"Of COURSE I'm in love with him," Trisha yelled. "And he was falling for me too until you came into the picture." Trisha growled and moved around, making Hope wonder what kind of weapon the woman was preparing now. "He might not have fallen as quick as I did, but he was on his way," Trisha muttered. "He would have come around. There's no way he could be that sweet and kind to me and not have feelings for me."

"So you tried to get rid of me by stealing? What's wrong with you?" Hope shouted. "Did you really think that would stick?"

Something else was broken and Hope began to worry that Trisha would destroy the entire house before she was done.

"When the stolen object was found in your room, it would have," Trisha muttered, sounding slightly distracted.

Hope's eyes grew wide. *Yeah...that probably would have done the trick.* "Then why didn't you do that with the ring?" she asked, hoping to keep Trisha talking. Hope peeked over the top of the bed to see Trisha fumbling with something in her hands. It was shiny, and fear unlike anything Hope had known came over her. She couldn't tell if Trisha had a knife or a gun, but it was obviously something dangerous.

"HANG ON, HOPE! I'M COMING!"

Both girls jerked their head toward the sound and Trisha dropped the weapon, which Hope could now see was a knife. As much as she wanted to wait for Enoch, who was banging on the wall behind her, Hope knew this was her best chance.

With a war cry for courage, she jumped from the floor and rushed Trisha, who screamed and clawed at Hope's face as they both fell to the ground. Hope squeezed her eyes shut and turned as Trisha's long nails met her cheek. Her skin immediately began to sting and liquid oozed down her cheek, letting Hope know she was bleeding.

Pushing the pain to the side, she fisted her hand and punched Trisha in the temple, temporarily stunning the woman. With Trisha not moving well, Hope scrambled off her and crawled on all fours to the knife, which she quickly threw across the room, away from Trisha and her machinations.

A loud bang from the wall brought Enoch scrambling into the room on his hands and knees through the small opening. "HOPE!" he bellowed, leaping forward and over Hope's head as he tackled Trisha to the floor once more.

Hope spun around and realized that Trisha had been aware enough to grab a vase and was about to hit Hope with it.

Enoch knocked the vase away and kept Trisha's hands pinned to the floor. His chest was heaving and he was covered in dirt and grime. "Hope! Hope, honey, are you okay?"

Hope nodded, then realized he wasn't facing her. She swallowed hard, her mouth dry. "Fine," she croaked. "Just dandy."

Enoch huffed. "Are you well enough to call the police? Or go have Bella do it?"

"LET ME GO!" Trisha screamed, her mascara running in large streaks down her cheeks as she cried. After a moment of confinement, she quit fighting Enoch's hold and simply sobbed. "It was supposed to be me," she rasped through her tears. "It was supposed to be me."

Enoch shook his head. "Hope? Can you get help?"

"What in this world?" Bella asked, opening the door to a hall full of faces.

"Bella, can you call the police, please?" Enoch said, his voice strained.

"I'm here," Hank, the detective said, stepping inside. He pulled a pair of handcuffs out of his back pocket and walked up to Enoch. "Just bring her hands in front here."

Enoch followed his directions and soon Trisha was being pulled to her feet and drug from the room, her wailing growing louder with every step.

Hope didn't move from her spot on the floor. She was such a wild mix of emotions at the moment that she wasn't sure which way to turn. Her heart was still racing like it was in a car chase, sweat and blood were trickling down her face and she could hardly catch her breath. *I can't believe everything was Trisha. How could she have done all this?* There was no time to answer her question, however, as the room began to fill with people.

ENOCH TURNED TO LOOK at her and his heart fell. "Oh my gosh, sweetheart. You're hurt." He hurried over and knelt beside her, reaching out to touch her cheek.

Hope grabbed his hand. "Are you okay?" she asked hoarsely.

He nodded. "Fine. Just dirty." He made a face. "And frightened out of my wits," he admitted sheepishly. "When I heard you scream, I was sure my heart had stopped."

Hope laughed a little, which quickly turned into tears, and she began to break down, giving Enoch the excuse to pull her into his arms. Their kneeling position was extremely awkward and he let himself fall back on his seat and then pulled her into his lap. "I've got ya," he said soothingly, rubbing her back, then her hair and kissing her head; anything he could think of to calm her down. "You're safe now, I have you." He continued to rub her back. "I love you," he whispered against her hair, closing his eyes at the image of her fight with Trisha. It wasn't something he would get rid of easily.

"She wanted me out of the way," Hope said through her tears. "She thought you would fall in love with her."

Enoch nodded sadly. "I know. I don't understand why she thought that, but I heard you two shouting at each other."

Hope raised her head. "She's crazy. She had a knife!"

Enoch felt another bout of fear strike him in the chest. "She had a knife? Where?"

Hope pointed to the other side of the room and Enoch followed her finger. She was right. A small pocket knife lay discarded in the corner and he had to swallow back the bile in his throat. There was obviously something very wrong with Trisha if she would resort to weapons like that to get Hope out of the way. Tucking Hope tighter into his chest, he buried his face in her hair and let all his emotions out. His body shook and his heart raced as the adrenaline in his system worked its way through his veins.

It was several minutes before he had control of himself again and could look up without feeling like he was going to throw up.

"Enoch?" Bella's voice was quiet and tentative, descriptions Enoch wouldn't normally associate with her.

He looked up to see her worried blue eyes trained on him and Hope.

"I'm sorry to break this up, but I think Hope needs medical attention on that cheek," Bella said.

"And the rest of us need an explanation," Claire called from the entrance to the room. She sighed loudly. "And I'll need to speak to the Mendelsons about the damage to their property."

"I think that's the least of our worries," Bella muttered.

"Says the girl who doesn't have to keep this inn running for the next twenty years," Claire snapped. Her eyes went to Enoch and softened. "Are you two all right?" she asked quietly.

Enoch nodded. "We will be."

Claire tsked her tongue and shook her head. "I was always slightly suspicious of her when she worked here, and now I know my instincts to not rehire her were correct." She took a deep breath. "Such a loss, though. She's so young."

Enoch looked down at Hope and the wounds on her cheek. "I think Bella's right. We need to get you taken care of."

Hope's hold on his back tightened. "I'm not ready to see anyone yet," she whispered. "I still can't seem to wrap my head around everything that happened. It's all a blur."

Enoch nodded understandingly. "I get it, but we don't want your cheek to get infected either. Let's just take care of one thing at a time, huh? Your cheek first. Then we'll worry about talking to Hank and Sheriff Davidson."

Hope chewed her lip for a second, then nodded. "You're right. My face stings like the devil, so it would probably be good to have someone look at it."

Enoch lifted her off his lap, just enough to stand, and then tucked her into his side again. "I'll be with you the whole way, okay?"

She nodded gratefully.

"An ambulance is on the way," Emory said from where she stood next to Antony. She played nervously with the phone in her hand, her eyes darting around as if she didn't know where to look.

Enoch hadn't realized half the town was here, although he shouldn't have been surprised. Antony seemed to be spending more and more time at the mansion and Enoch was positive it had nothing to do with the building of the gingerbread village.

He nodded at Emory. "Thanks. I'll take her downstairs."

Emory nodded. She stepped forward as if to speak to Hope, only to step back again, Antony's hand on her lower back. "We're here, Hope," she finally offered.

Hope acknowledged her cousin, but didn't let go of her grip on Enoch, for which he was grateful. Seeing her wounded and being attacked had been more than his heart could take, and he wasn't quite ready to share her with anyone yet, although he knew he probably should. *I'm sure Claire wants to check on her granddaughter, but I just can't bring myself to let go yet.*

And it appeared as if Hope felt the same way, if her clinging was anything to go by. He guided her down the stairs and sat them on a bench in the foyer, waiting for the authorities to arrive.

It only took a few minutes for there to be a pounding on the door. Enoch stood to answer it, but Hope clung to his hand.

"I got it," Bella called out, hurrying down the last couple of steps. "You just sit tight," she said to Enoch and Hope.

"Thanks," Enoch said, sitting back down and putting his arm around Hope.

"I don't want to go to the hospital," Hope whispered to him.

"You don't have to if you don't want to," Enoch assured her, rubbing her upper arm. "It'll be all right."

She sighed. "I'm sorry I'm being such a baby. I really should stand on my own two feet, but I feel so…lost, I guess. I've dealt with bullies and mean women before, but this was so much more." Hope shook her head. "I never would have guessed that these kinds of things happen in real life."

"I know," Enoch murmured. "And I'm sorry. I had no idea she was mentally unstable."

"It's not your fault—" Hope began before they were interrupted by a paramedic.

"Miss?" he said. "Can I take a look at your cheek?"

Hope sighed and nodded. "Thanks," she said to the first responder, who nodded in return.

"Looks like you're going to need a few stitches," he stated after pushing around on her cheek for a bit.

"Can we do that here?" Hope asked. "I don't want to leave."

The paramedic shook his head. "I'd really recommend going in. Especially since this is on your face, you're going to want it done by someone with more skills than me or my partner. There might even be a surgeon on hand to make any scarring as light as possible."

Hope sighed and Enoch waited for her to make a decision. "Fine," she answered, then looked to Enoch. "I hate to ask it, but would you be willing to come? I'm not ready to be alone yet."

Enoch kissed her forehead. "There's nowhere else I'd rather be."

CHAPTER 16

Hope looked at the tiny stitches in her cheek the next morning and winced at her reflection. Her cheek was swollen and bruised and covered in dark x's from the threads. "Like Enoch will want to spend time with me now," she muttered.

She glanced at the clock. *Speaking of Enoch...* She needed to speak to him about those three little words he threw into their conversation yesterday. *Were they just spur of the moment, or did he actually mean it?*

Hope had known she was in love with Enoch for a while, but she figured it was far too soon to expect the same from him. At least she had thought so until it had spilled from his lips yesterday.

She'd been so shell-shocked and fragile yesterday that she hadn't even thought to bring anything up with him after the hospital visit. By the time they'd gotten back, Hope had been exhausted and gone to bed early.

But now Hope was up, and her mind was much clearer. "And I want to know if he truly meant it," she murmured to herself in the mirror. She touched her wound again, grimacing at the picture she made, but knowing standing around wasn't going to make it any better. Forcing herself to move, she got dressed and headed downstairs to help with breakfast.

"Oh!" Hope cried softly when she got to the kitchen. To say it was full was an understatement. Sheriff Davidson, Detective Gordon, Enoch and all of the women were there. Hope glanced at her cell phone. "Did I sleep in and not realize it?"

"Of course not," Grandma Claire said primly. "Everyone simply came over to get things settled this morning." She patted the chair next to her at the table. "Come. Sit."

Hope's eyes caught Enoch's as she walked to her grandmother's side, and she gave him a tentative smile.

His compassionate gaze moved over her injury like a caress before she met his eyes. "Good morning," he whispered.

"Good morning," she said back.

"You can cuddle later," Grandma Claire declared. "Come sit down."

Hope felt her cheeks go hot, adding to the burn from the stitches, as everyone else chuckled. She stepped past Enoch, and he let his fingers slide along hers, giving her a much needed boost in the face of so much embarrassment. Slipping into the chair next to Grandma Claire, she glared at her grandma. "Was that really necessary?"

Grandma Claire gave her a dry look. "He had you all to himself yesterday. It's time the rest of your family got a chance." She reached out and took Hope's chin, turning her head one way, then the other before tsking her tongue. "That woman deserves whatever is coming to her."

Hope pulled away. "That *woman* is obviously not right in the head, Grandma."

"Still..." Grandma Claire turned to Detective Gordon. "What can you tell us?"

The detective cleared his throat and pulled a notebook out of his jacket pocket. "It's not a pretty story." His dark eyes met Hope's. "Are you sure you want to hear it?"

Hope swallowed, then nodded. Somewhere along the line Trisha had been wronged and Hope wanted to know why.

"Trisha Finley. Female, age—"

"Hank," Bella snapped. "Really?"

The detective gave her a small scowl. "Did you want to hear what I have written down or not?"

"Only the pertinent information," Bella retorted. "We all know she was a woman."

He sighed and flipped a couple of pages. "During her interrogation last night, Trisha admitted to using the secret passageways to steal the ring, messing with the cleaning cart..." He frowned. "Throwing towels on the floor?"

Hope nodded. "Yeah. I had to rewash them."

The detective made a face. "Okay... she also said she had been planning to steal something else from the Mendelsons' room, then plant it in Hope's." He snapped his notebook shut and looked at Hope. "She wanted you out of the way so lover boy over there would date her instead."

"She said as much when we were fighting," Hope agreed. "Was there anything else? She didn't seem stable."

Detective Gordon nodded. "She's undergoing an evaluation soon. But that was pretty much all we got out of her. She thought she and Enoch were an item until you came along and messed it all up."

"We were never together," Enoch said, his tone slightly guttural. His body was tense and his jaw clenched. It was easy to see he was more than frustrated at the situation.

Detective Gordon put up his hand. "I believe you. We tried asking why she thought you were together, and all we could get from her was that you were nice to her." He smirked. "I don't really count that as declaring a relationship."

Enoch snorted, but his body language loosened and he relaxed a little.

"Wait a minute," Emory said, stepping in. "What about all the other stuff?"

The detective frowned. "I tried asking her about the missing food, but she didn't seem to know what I was talking about." He shrugged. "While I do believe there's an illness going on, she was competent enough to speak plainly to the officers interrogating her."

Emory's mouth drooped. "But I *know* someone took my candy and pie. Plus, fruit and baking chips have disappeared as well."

"Crap!" Enoch shouted. "I can't believe I forgot." He began to walk out of the kitchen. "Hang on a sec."

Everyone looked to Hope while he was gone, but she shrugged. "I have no idea what's going on," she admitted.

They heard Enoch running up the stairs and then down again a couple minutes later before he popped back into the kitchen with a pie plate in his hands.

"My pie!" Emory cried, rushing forward. She grabbed the dish. "I *knew* it." She turned and held it up. "I told you someone took my pie. And they ate it just like they did my nougat."

Detective Gordon stepped forward. "Where did you find that?" he asked Enoch.

"When I was walking around in the walls, I ended up in a hidden attic," Enoch explained. "There were a bunch of blankets, an old pair of boots and a small table." He pointed to the pie plate. "That was on the table."

"So someone's living in the attic?" Bella asked, her voice more excited than Hope's would have been.

Hope shivered and sunk into her seat. "Why am I getting the feeling that our problems haven't ended with Trisha?"

Detective Gordon scribbled something in his notebook and stuffed it in his pocket. "It seems like you're right, Ms. Hope. I think we have more than one person causing trouble around here."

"Oh my gosh, this is exciting," Bella gushed. "And here I thought it would all end with the crazy lady behind bars."

Hope groaned and let her forehead rest on the table. "I'm not up for any more excitement," she said. "I just wanted a peaceful Christmas with family. Is that too much to ask?"

"Apparently so," Emory said, her voice sharp. "And I still want to know who is trying to sabotage me."

ENOCH TUNED OUT HANK as he began asking Emory questions. Antony had stepped up and was inserting his own opinions, but none of it revolved around Hope, so he ventured over to the table.

"Hey," he said softly, slipping into the seat beside her. She looked exhausted and her injury looked painful. He hurt for her and felt the stirring of anger in his chest as he thought of what Trisha did. Taking a deep breath, Enoch tried to push the feelings away. *She's sick,* he reminded himself. *She wasn't making clear choices.*

Despite understanding that something was wrong with the woman, Enoch found it difficult to reconcile his logic with his heart. The woman he loved had been hurt, and he wanted to hurt the person who had done it.

"Hey," Hope whispered back, straightening up from the table. She studied him. "Are you doing okay this morning?"

Enoch nodded. "Don't worry about me," he said, brushing a hair from her forehead. "I'm not the one who got hurt."

Hope shrugged. "I'll live." She frowned. "Although I'm vain enough to admit that I hope it doesn't scar. I may not be the prettiest flower in the garden, but I wasn't looking to add a mark right across my cheekbone."

Enoch glared. "Are you really trying to tell me that the woman I love isn't beautiful?" He'd told her last night that he loved her, but everything had been so hurried that nothing more had been said. However, after yesterday's disaster, Enoch didn't want to waste any more time between them.

Hope's eyes misted over. "About that..."

Enoch shook his head. "Not here." He stood and offered his hand. "Come on. Let's go find somewhere quiet."

"You need to eat!" Claire called after them, ruining Enoch's plan of a stealthy getaway.

Hope rolled her eyes. "I will, Grandma. Give me a bit."

They tried to leave again, but Bella stopped them.

"Hey, Hope?"

"Yeah?"

Bella winked. "I'll clean the rooms for you today. Why don't you take a little time off?"

Enoch couldn't help but chuckle and shake his head.

"I think I'll take you up on that," Hope said with a smile. "Thank you."

Bella smirked, looking very pleased with herself. "You're welcome." Her eyes darted to Hank, who was still talking. "Just don't forget to return the favor someday."

"Oh good heavens," Hope whispered under her breath as Enoch walked them out of the room. "Where are we going?" she asked as he helped her put on a jacket.

"My apartment," Enoch explained. "No one will bother us there."

"Sounds like heaven," Hope sighed, walking with him outside. "Ooh, it's cold."

"It's December," he said with a laugh.

"I know, but still..."

Enoch chuckled and hurried her across to the garage and then upstairs.

"There we go," he said, taking her coat. "Nice and warm."

"Perfect," she gushed, walking over to put her hands over his fireplace.

Enoch fiddled with the coat for a moment, gathering his courage. He watched her stand by the fireplace, so beautiful but so fragile in the soft light. His heart fluttered a little and he knew he couldn't keep putting it off. "I meant what I said earlier, you know."

"What was that?" Hope asked over her shoulder.

"That I didn't like you talking derogatory about the woman I love."

Hope stiffened slightly and then turned to look at him. "Enoch..."

He walked purposefully toward her, taking her hands in his. "I know we haven't been together long, Hope, but I can't deny how I feel." He squeezed her cold and trembling fingers. "I love you. I started falling in love with you from the moment I saw you right after Thanksgiving, and each..." He stepped closer, swallowing hard. "Each touch, each kiss, each time you smiled..." Enoch shook his head. "Only made me fall harder. You bring peace to my life and happiness to my days." Enoch blinked rapidly, his emotions getting the better of him. "I think when you so easily accepted my past with my dad was when I knew for sure that we had something special. But it wasn't until Trisha hurt you that I knew I couldn't hold it inside anymore." He slowly wrapped his hands around her waist, pulling her into his chest, and rested his forehead against hers, taking a moment to breathe her in. "I love you," he whispered.

"Enoch..." she said breathlessly, leaning back to put her hands on his cheeks. "I love you too...so much!"

Pure unadulterated joy sprung up inside Enoch and he wasted no time in bringing his mouth to hers in celebration. His grip on her back tightened and he rejoiced when her hands went into his hair, tugging and playing, generally driving him crazy. He couldn't get enough of her and he knew his vision of their life together was eventually going to come true.

Finally, Hope pulled back, breathing heavily. "For the first time since I got here, I'm actually too warm," she said with a grin.

Enoch jumped, realizing she was still up against the fireplace. "Why didn't you say something?" he scolded, pulling her over to the couch and promptly tugging her into his lap.

"I did," she said, her tone happy and light.

He laughed. "We could have burned you."

"But we didn't."

"But—"

Hope put a finger over his lips. "No buts," she stated firmly. "Don't ruin this moment for me."

He smiled, grabbing her fingers and kissing them. "Is that a polite way of saying 'shut up and kiss me'?"

Hope grinned. "I didn't say that, but I'm not about to argue with it either."

"That makes two of us," he managed to say before they continued their celebration for a good long while.

Later, when they were lazily relaxing on the couch with a movie playing in the background, Enoch stirred enough to say something that had been on his mind. "Hope?"

"Hmm?"

He played with her hair as her head rested on his chest. "Now that I've found you, I'm not sure I'm ready to be separated."

"We aren't," she said with a yawn.

"What I mean is...I don't think I want you to leave after Christmas. Would you ever consider working around here?" He felt her shift against him and Enoch hoped he hadn't gone too far. Saying they loved each other was wonderful, but many people did long distance relationships. However, Enoch didn't want to be one of them. "I know it's not your big city with all the amenities, but Seagull Cove has some nice points to it as well."

Hope propped herself against his chest so she could see his eyes. "There really isn't anything keeping me in Utah," she said softly. "I don't have a permanent job and although I enjoy the city, I don't have my heart set on it." She patted his chest. "My heart is right here. And provided I can find work in the area, I don't see why it would be a big deal."

"Just like that?" he asked, surprised she'd given in so easily. It was a big decision and he wouldn't have blamed her if she wanted to think about it for a while.

Hope shrugged and settled back against him. "If it makes you feel better, I'll hang onto my apartment lease, just in case, but there's nothing holding me there, Enoch. My whole heart seems to be at the Gingerbread Inn."

Enoch kissed the top of her head in wonder and awe. He never would have imagined that Claire's accident would have led to the best thing in Enoch's life. The woman in his arms was amazing and everything he could have ever dreamed of. And when the time was right, he knew that he would make her choice to move to Seagull Cove a permanent one. But for now...he would love her and convince her that small town life was everything she could ever want.

EPILOGUE

Enoch adjusted the chair. Stepped back, then adjusted it again.

"It's fine!" Bella scolded him. She slapped his hands and pushed him away from the rocking chair. "You need to chill."

Enoch glared. "Maybe I would if you would back off."

Bella gave him a look. "You asked for my help, remember? It's your fault that I'm here helping you set up a proposal."

He pushed his hands through his hair. "You're right. I'm a mess."

"So is every man before he shackles himself for life," she drawled.

"Not helping!" Enoch nearly shouted.

She grinned sweetly. "It wasn't meant to."

"Maybe I shouldn't do this," he snapped. "I'm not sure I want you as a cousin-in-law."

"At least Hope and I don't live together." Bella shuddered. "Can you imagine all I'd have to put up with if that was the case? You two are mushier than a Hallmark movie."

"Okay." Enoch headed to his front door and opened it. "I think you've done your job. Thank you."

She gaped at him. "Are you kicking me out? And before the good part?"

"Yes."

Bella hmphed and stalked across the room. "See if I help you with any more proposals," she huffed as she walked down the stairs.

"Considering I don't plan to do this again, I don't think that'll be a problem."

"Yeah, well...I hope she says yes, then. Or we'll be having another talk, huh?"

"Goodbye, Bella" he called out, slamming the door behind her. Enoch rested his hands on the door for a minute to catch his breath. He loved Hope's family, but sometimes the cousins were a bit too much.

Straightening, he looked around the room and had to give grudging credit where it was due. The flowers, chocolates and other decorations looked pretty darn good.

Footsteps on the stairs caught his attention and his breath caught. "Okay, okay. This is it. You've been planning for this. Stay calm and it'll all work out."

"Enoch?"

He threw open the door. "Merry Christmas two days late!" he said too loudly, then winced. "Since you were working Christmas day, I was hoping we could celebrate now," he explained.

Hope laughed and stepped into his apartment with a welcome kiss. "That sounds wonderful. Merry Christmas to you," she whispered against his lips. Turning away from him, she groaned and threw her head back. "You wouldn't believe the day I've had. The inn is full and so I had to clean everything." Hope unwrapped her scarf. "Mr. Theodore is the pickiest person I have ever met." She paused and looked at Enoch. "Did you know that there's only one way to clean a toilet?"

"Uh…"

"Well, according to him, there is, and I don't do it." She sighed and threw her scarf over a kitchen chair before pausing. "Enoch…" Her wide blue eyes took in the room. "Oh my gosh. Here I was complaining and you put all this together."

He came up behind her and wrapped his arms around her waist before kissing her cheek. The one where a small, white scar sat delicately a little below her eye. "I was hoping you would join me for a nice evening," he whispered in her ear.

She spun in his arms. "That sounds wonderful," she said, wrapping her arms around his neck. "I…" She froze, then slowly turned back around. "Enoch…isn't that the rocker from downstairs?"

Enoch pushed her toward the chair and stopped them right in front of it. "Do you like it?" he asked.

She nodded. "I love it. You know that."

"Remember when you told me you would buy it from me?"

She nodded again.

"Well, I've finally decided to sell it."

She turned with a gasp. "You said you wouldn't."

"And I know what I want in exchange."

She opened and closed her mouth a couple of times, then her eyes misted over. "What have you decided?"

"I've decided only one thing will do." He let go of her and reached into his back pocket, grabbing the velvet box before stepping back and dropping to one knee. "Hope Lynn Masterson," he began. "I love you. I've loved you since I laid eyes on you back just after Thanksgiving. I love your sweetness, your acceptance, your smiles, your laughter, you kisses and your kind heart. I love how you help out your grandmother at the inn, even though it isn't what you want for a career. I love that you smile and help Bella even when she drives you crazy. I love that you encourage everyone around you, no matter how different from you they are. I love how your face lights up when you're happy, and I love how you bring that happiness into my life. I was content before you arrived, but you've changed that. You've made me want more. Much more." Enoch took a deep breath. "I don't want to say goodnight to you. I want to wake up and say good morning instead. I don't want to brush your fingers in passing at the inn. I want to hold you all day long. I don't want to call you Hope Masterson. I want you to be Hope Dunlap. And...I don't want that rocking chair to sit downstairs anymore. I want it up here, where you can sit on it every day. Where you'll eventually rock our babies to sleep and sing lullabies that win over the heart of every person in hearing."

Tears were streaming down her cheeks, but Enoch pushed ahead, hoping they were happy tears.

"So in exchange for the use of that chair, I'm asking for you, Hope. I'm asking for your heart, your time and your future as well. Most of all, I'm asking if you'll be my wife."

His knee was cramping against the wooden boards and Enoch shifted a little, feeling terrified of what would come next. He knew Hope loved him, but they hadn't been together all that long, at least not by the world's standards. But he wasn't asking the world to marry him. He was asking Hope. Now he just had to hope she was ready.

"I have a confession." She sniffed, wiping at her cheeks.

Fear thudded through his chest.

"I sold my apartment lease."

He frowned. "What? When?"

Hope shook her head and tugged him to his feet. "As soon as you asked me to stay."

Enoch's jaw went slack. "Why?"

"Because I had a Christmas wish that wouldn't stop running through my head," she said with a small grin. "Instead of the usual scarf or perfume, I wanted something very specific." Her grin grew. "I wanted a handyman. And it appears that my wish was heard."

Enoch shook his head, then slipped the solitaire onto her finger. "You amaze me."

"And you are everything I've ever wanted."

Enoch took his time cherishing every bit of her and letting her know without words how happy he was with her agreement. Time had become irrelevant when they finally came up for air.

"It was the chair, wasn't it?" he asked as he kissed along her jawline. "That was what made you agree."

She laughed breathlessly. "Of course. I've always been in it for the rocker."

Enoch turned the two of them, sat down in the chair and pulled her into his lap. "Then I think maybe it's time we start making some memories with it," he said, cupping her face. "Because it's going to be with us for a really long time."

I just adore Happy Endings!
And sweet men like Enoch are
definitely my kryptonite!
Not ready for the romance to be over?
Don't worry!
Emory's story is up next in
"Her Christmas Baker"

Other Books by Laura Ann

<u>THE GINGERBREAD INN</u> [1]
<u>"Her Christmas Handyman"</u>[2]
<u>"Her Christmas Baker"</u>[3]
<u>"Her Christmas Detective"</u>[4]
SAGEBRUSH RANCH
When city girls meet cowboys,
All sorts of fun ensues.
<u>Books 1-6</u>[5]
LOCKWOOD INDUSTRIES
The Lockwood triplets started a personal security business.
Little did they know it would double as a matchmaking business!
<u>Books 1-6</u>[6]
OVERNIGHT BILLIONAIRE BACHELORS
Three brothers become overnight billionaires.
Will they discover that love is the real treasure?
<u>Books 1-5</u>[7]
IT'S ALL ABOUT THE MISTLETOE
When 6 friends brings fake dates to their high school reunion,
mayhem and mistletoe win the day!

---

1. https://www.amazon.com/gp/product/B08N4JD51P?ref_=dbs_p_mng_rwt_ser_shvlr&store-Type=ebooks

2. https://www.amazon.com/dp/B08MZ3NKRM

3. https://www.amazon.com/dp/B08N4Q5KH2

4. https://www.amazon.com/dp/B08N3NKDHK

5. https://www.amazon.com/gp/product/B089YPCF6X?ref_=dbs_r_series&storeType=ebooks

6. https://www.amazon.com/gp/product/B083Z49VL3?ref_=dbs_r_series&storeType=ebooks

7. https://www.amazon.com/gp/product/B07RJZL29J?ref_=dbs_r_series&storeType=ebooks

<u>Books 1-6</u>[8]
MIDDLETON PREP
If you enjoy fairy tale romance,
these sweet, contemporary retellings are for you!
<u>Books 1-9</u>[9]

8. https://www.amazon.com/gp/product/B082F8FTHY?ref_=dbs_r_series&storeType=ebooks

9. https://www.amazon.com/gp/product/B07DYCWRQL?ref_=dbs_r_series&store-
   Type=ebooks

CPSIA information can be obtained
at www.ICGtesting.com
Printed in the USA
FSHW021256091121
86088FS